THE LOVE SURVEY

THE LOVE SURVEY

MORTON COOPER

CUTTING EDGE

ISBN-13: 978-1-962896-47-4

Published by
Cutting Edge Books
PO Box 8212
Calabasas, CA 91372
www.cuttingedgebooks.com

CHAPTER ONE

❧ ❧ ❧

THE CHAPEL was clean and quiet, and the tones were properly hushed, but, thought Phil Morrow as the mournful usher guided him to where the others sat, it had about as much innate dignity as a dance hall. The redhead who had chewed gum as she took his hat belonged not in a funeral home but at a faro table, cadging the Alaska miners for more redeye. The usher, with his patently phony expression of fervent sympathy, was right out of Central Casting. The canned organ music segued from "Oh, What a Beautiful Morning" to "Always."

Everything about the chapel seemed cynically rented for the occasion, strictly cash and carry, let's snap this up fellas because there are more stiffs waiting for theirs in the next room and we're already a half-hour behind.

Dr. Alders, who lay in the plain box up at the curtain of the stage, had been more or less indifferent to religion and to excessively solemn services of any kind, and he would have been the first to wave his fine hand at any moist formalities prior to cremation. But he had been a worthy man, a man of unflagging quality, and he deserved more than this side show send-off.

Phil Morrow, whom Dr. Alders had tabbed to take over the Alders Institute Survey on Sex Conduct before Sunday's fatal heart attack at the press conference in Marston City, took his place in the fourth-row pew beside Mike Crayne and Nelson

Partridge. They appeared as uncomfortable as he. Nancy Garrity, the newest member of the team of interviewers, was missing, but Phil hadn't expected to see her here. Three hours ago she had come to his and Mike's suite at the Hotel St. Charles, hemmed and hawed a little more than was called for, and asked to be excused from the service. "I can be a tower of strength anywhere except at funerals," she'd said. "Will it be awful if I'm a coward and just wait here?"

They had understood and told her to stay put.

There were fewer than a hundred people in the high-backed pews now, not because the chapel couldn't have been filled beyond capacity with those who honestly mourned Dr. Alders' passing, but because Mrs. Alders, otherwise wispy and painfully shy, insisted that the service be as simple and uncluttered as possible. Phil recognized a handful of the celebrities, the earnest scientists in the field of sex research, the absolute giants, and he was impressed that they had come. Fiedler and Armstrong and Barry made this city, Victor Alders' city, their home base, but Rothschild surely had flown 2,000 miles to be here. Here and there were other giants and quasi-giants in the field and in related fields, colleagues and admirers of Dr. Alders. Toward the rear of the stuffy room was Eli Griffiths Soren, the worshiped mountain. He had been against Dr. Alders' methods over the past half-dozen years, and they had met in virulent debate more than once. But Soren had seen fit to be on deck, and Phil was certain that Dr. Alders, who recoiled from any sign of suspect sentiment, would have been openly delighted.

The cleric who had been hired to conduct the show emerged from the wings after "Always" was finished, and made his way on short legs to the podium overlooking the coffin. His name, the chapel folks had told Phil and Mrs. Alders, was Bertram Willard, and he was in demand partly because he had worked his way through divinity school by touring in summers with Maurice Evans. Those who mourned here the second and third time around invariably asked for Reverend Williard because he spoke so comfortingly.

At the podium, he removed his glasses, pinched the bridge of his nose studiedly with his thumb and forefinger, surveyed his audience as though he were counting the house, and waited for total silence. When it was given, he shot his cuffs and viewed his notes.

"We are assembled here on this grievous day," he intoned in a voice carved out of molten butter, "to swiftly but genuinely deliver our heartfelt farewells to a man who was convinced of his purpose, as are how many of us? Victor Ekhardt Alders, born and raised in our city, was not one of your garret scientists who chose to be one of your, ah, absent-minded professors and devote his life to dissecting worms. Victor Alders, ever vibrant and mindful of perhaps the holiest of all creations, the life force, chose to clasp hands with the greats of mankind and to study, for all of us to know, what makes man tick. As it were."

Where in hell, or heaven, did they find this patronizing creep? Phil wondered. Next to him, Mike Crayne winced and young Nelson Partridge crossed and uncrossed his legs unhappily. If a scene wouldn't be guaranteed, Phil was sure he would have risen and walked out, as he knew men like Rothschild and Soren would have. The fatuous cleric, who had never known Dr. Alders' work and was sweating to avoid mentioning the dirty word *sex*, was a torment. Surely the timid Mrs. Alders and her obviously nice children in the front row had sensed as much after the initial moment.

Doctor, Phil thought, I will switch off this sober master of ceremonies' spiel and deliver my own swift but genuine eulogy.

Doc, you were no prize to work for. When you wanted to be, you could be nasty and a bit of a prima donna. We would start to talk after working hours about different techniques in interviewing Americans on their sex lives, and if I only passingly rubbed you the wrong way you were a terror, as miserably self-sure as that jolly round potato with the turned collar up there at stage center.

But Doc, Dr. Alders, you were one hell of a man. You were a bigger giant than all the rest of them, and even that fathead with his horrid patronizing speech won't make people forget you. You had compassion enough and brilliance enough to last over generations, and sixty-four was far too young to die.

You are going to be missed.

"—and although those of us who unashamedly consider ourselves among the more conservative may occasionally question the propriety of some of his methods, we can appreciate that Dr. Alders, for whatever scientific reasons he divined—"

Phil Morrow was a lankily tall man of thirty-three who was acutely conscious of the fact that he looked at least five years younger. His long, unlined face was resolutely alive rather than handsome, and he had the knack of being able to wear the most disheveled clothes and yet have a responsible critic call him well dressed. He had long, steady, plastic fingers. He had never married.

Today he was worried.

The press would be waiting for him back at the hotel. He had promised to fill them in on how the sex surveys were going to be changed now that he was in charge, and he would have to select his words carefully. Any misunderstood criticisms of Dr. Alders' techniques would immediately dub him, Phil, an upstart, and he had enough to contend with as it was without inviting the newspapers and news magazines to brand him as an opportunist—and a baby-faced, unequipped one, at that.

There was no grave question of his credentials, of course; the Doctor had made it clear often enough in public that, despite certain basic disagreements between them, Morrow was his unequivocal choice for the next in line, and Mrs. Alders gladly seconded the choice. But the responsibilities were tremendous, and one solidly false move could bring chaos to a project which

Victor Alders, over a period of years and backbreaking work, had honed to an artful smoothness. The problem of persuading men and women throughout the country to air the most secret compartments of their lives had not been solved overnight. The national acceptance of the project had taken an arduously hard, long time and, Phil was sharply aware, imperfect administration or the dimmest hint of scandal could destroy it.

Hardly the least of the upcoming barrel of problems rested with the researchers who traveled together from one city to another. Crayne, Partridge and Nancy Garrity knew their stuff, but at least a half-dozen more trained people were needed. Dr. Alders had known this and was always planning to add more interviewers, but never got to it. His sudden death last Sunday, among the other disruptions it incurred, wasn't about to encourage an addition to the team in a hurry.

And Phil Morrow knew he would need help. Of the three others, only Mike Crayne understood, or could be brought around to understand and agree to, the change of emphasis in the survey that was to come. Partridge and Garrity were competent statisticians and were considerably more flexible than most of the young psychologists available, but neither had been trained in anything but the most rudimentary edges of psychotherapy and neither had undergone personal analysis or therapy. They would stay on for the time being. Afterwards, once the new regime began to move without kinks, and when he was satisfied that Crayne had fully come around to his thinking, they would concentrate on hiring the bigger fish, the psychotherapists.

The dream took active form again in his mind. The Alders Survey composed entirely of mature psychologists who were trained therapists.

The whole circumspect field, so eager to light up the pitchy corners and be progressive that it was always a good twenty years behind the times, would bowl over on cue. The psychiatrists, even the far-seeing ones who favored group therapy, would write rambling letters to the medical journals full of protest and archaic vocabulary.

But all that would pass. The plan was an excellent one because it was a natural one. The graphs and charts and slide rules had their rightful place in the project, but they amounted only to a small bandage on a thousand-fingered hand.

Now. How do you say that to the press without having all the blue-haired old ladies yell for the cops?

The actor-cleric finished his performance and the audience filed out as the canned organ played a dirgeful "How Deep Is the Ocean?" Dr. Alders had specifically ordered his wife to have him cremated immediately following the service and to see that everyone left the chapel right after the final Amens.

Mrs. Alders, looking tiny and confused in the outer lobby, was surrounded by family Phil had either never or briefly met. She spotted him and excused herself from the crowd. Phil had been with Dr. Alders from the time shortly after graduate school and had heard him say, more than once, "This life is a far cry from the invention of the family, isn't it, Phil? I have the best wife on earth and I almost never see her. Sometimes I can't draw a picture of her in my mind." Phil had met her maybe a half-dozen times over the years. Each time she had struck him as an extremely fine woman.

"That service was an atrocity, Philip, but I'm glad you and the others came," she said, more composed than he would have expected. She placed her little, chubby hands into his, and he had the feeling she would have been free enough to weep in his arms if there had been privacy.

"May I take you home, Mrs. Alders?"

"You're meeting the reporters, aren't you?"

"They can wait."

"I wouldn't think of it. The children have the car and they suggested we take a drive through the country before going back home. It sounds like a good idea. I want to get home—but not right away."

"Of course."

"How long will you be in town, Philip?" she asked.

"Just another day or two, I think. We're expected in Waymouth on the fourteenth and there's a lot of work to be done ahead of time."

"There's one thing I would appreciate, though, if you can find the time. But only if it's convenient."

"Name it, Mrs. Alders."

"Would you come visit us sometime before you leave? The Doctor spoke so highly of you that we came to consider you one of the family. I'd ask the others to come with you—Dr. Crayne and the others—but I think at this point—"

"Certainly. I'll come this evening. I'll phone first."

On his way to the gum-chewing girl at the checkroom, where Mike and Nelson waited for him, Phil was approached by Dr. Rothschild who called him by name. He had met the eminent Rothschild only once, four or five years ago, through Dr. Alders, and was agreeably surprised that the man remembered him. He waited now and shook the lumbering man's hand.

"I won't hold you up now, Morrow," he said, frowning under a forest of violent black eyebrows, a six-foot, six-inch behemoth with craggy features that were duck soup to sketch. "My plane leaves for Chicago at nine tonight. Would you be free to have dinner or a drink with me?"

It was Einstein inviting a high-school physics student for a friendly meeting of the minds.

"I certainly would, sir. How's—let's see—half-past six?"

"That sounds all right."

"I'm at the St. Charles," Phil said. "We could—"

"I'm stopping at the Vanderton House. That's about eight or ten blocks from your hotel. I'll see you in the lobby at six-thirty on the dot."

"Good. Ah—which lobby? Yours or mine?"

Rothschild blinked. "Mine," he answered, in the voice he must have used when he talked to children.

The taxi driver who drove Phil, Nelson and Mike back to the St. Charles wasn't nearly so snarled in traffic as he pretended, and the meter was clicking with uncommon speed, but they were too drained to make an issue of the too tranquil pace. Phil and Mike ached for a drink. Nelson Partridge, who was twenty-eight, who rarely talked, and whom Mike had privately and rather accurately called the world's oldest adolescent, doubtless would escape to his own hotel room and the safety of his thoughts as soon as they were let out.

Phil decided it was just as well. Nelson, for all his shows of being the Milquetoast village square, was an exceptionally smart young man and had been one of Dr. Alders' most promising biology students at Harthley, but he was undeniably something of an odd ball, certainly not someone to lazily shoot the breeze with. Mike Crayne had his own dark areas of complexity, too, but he was distinctly easy company, Phil's age, and more outgoing than the rest of the team, and Phil was fond of him. He was a little shorter than the other two men, chiefly because he slouched, but his eyes were constantly alert and he gave the impression of great physical strength. He had been with Dr. Alders exactly a year less than had Phil Morrow. The Doctor had come across him at the Yalebrough Clinic, where he had been doing apparently out-standing work in psychological testing. Phil assumed from subtle bits and snatches of conversation that he was separated from his wife, but he volunteered little information and Phil didn't prod.

The afternoon was unreasonably warm for May, the men agreed as the cab pulled up toward the sufficiently cosmopolitan hotel and discharged them. The radio weatherman had announced the day would be pleasant, but the men knew differently. It was going to be a hot day, and that promised them the season would be hot. It was past three o'clock but the sun was still scowling down, sucking the moisture from the earth.

"I defer to no man in my love for the Doc," Mike sighed just before the gold-braided doorman admitted them to the mammoth lobby, "but he sure could've learned a lot more about scheduling. New York State in the summer!" he cursed and relieved himself of a discreet but nasty throat gurgle. "December's the only time of the year civilized people should go to New York. I spent twelve happily cold summers in New Hampshire. I should've told him people sleep together in New Hampshire, too."

Nelson blanched and looked to see if anyone had heard.

In the main lobby, the assistant manager named Starbuck strode forward and greeted them. "Dr. Morrow, I sent the reporters up to the suite's living room, like you asked me."

"Thank you." The assistant manager, ten years ago before fashions had changed, likely had worn striped pants and an enormous lapel carnation. The men had never seen him before yesterday afternoon when they had hurriedly flown to this city, but he seemed naked and bereft without the uniform.

"I do hope your quarters are satisfactory, gentlemen," Starbuck dribbled hopefully as they worked their ways toward the open elevator.

"Everything's satisfactory," Phil lied. The quarters were lousy. They had been assured by Herb Graham, the Survey's advance man, that the St. Charles was one of the three best hotels in the city, that the neighborhood was unbeatable, that even movie stars stayed here regularly. It was not a good hotel.

"Do they allow intoxicating beverages in their satisfactory rooms?" Mike asked as the elevator ascended.

"If they don't, and if the walls are wired for sound," Phil replied, "we're as good as in the electric chair. My attache case is bulging with an unopened bottle of gin."

"You asked me, so I'm telling you," Mike Crayne said, rubbing his forehead with one hand as he held a drink in the other. He was sensitive about losing his hair, and unconsciously, during conversations, he rubbed fingers into his scalp as he talked. "You're making a mistake. You want to do more than gather statistics, the way the Doc did, and compile them neatly and publish them and let the public buy and read and judge and take in. You want not only to interview these sexless or sexed-up matrons, you want to give them treatment, as well."

"It's not as simple as that," Phil protested.

"Those goblins in the next room will think it is, and they'll race to their city desks like Torquemada. And so what's the difference? You're a bright guy, professor, and I'm a bright guy. I'm signing on for another hitch, and I'll bow to your wishes because, of us two bright guys, you're the brighter. I can say that here and now without fear of being struck dumb. You're brighter."

"Cut that crap."

"No crap. What I'm telling you is that you're treading a dangerous path. You can't listen to men's and women's sex histories and personalize with treatment at the same time. It's like laying a stripper and reading Sartre simultaneously. Sartre won't get completely read and the stripper'll get on your back—or somebody's back—for rebates. Who's helped?"

"Everybody's helped. I didn't wait for Alders to die to initiate this plan. He knew all about it. He disagreed with me, but not enough to kick me out. You were around through the whole discussion. If he thought I was the mad scientist from Karloff Hill he wouldn't've put me next in line."

"I get it," Mike said. "Li'l ol' Crayne's getting the upperechelon bit."

"Oh, Christ, drop it, Shirley Temple! Let's not hurt its wittle feelwings at this stage of the game. You know what I mean."

"Do I?" Mike asked, his leg flung carelessly over the arm of the chair nearest the window.

The press was waiting in the next room, drinking the Institute's drinks, smoking the Institute's cigars and cigarettes, and eating the Institute's canapés and salami sandwiches, but Phil and Mike had felt the need for a breather, a drink, a shower, a change of clothes, and another drink. Nelson had shifted from one gangling foot to another in the bedroom as Phil had unlocked the gin, had exchanged a few meaningless words, and then had darted off to his own single room on the next floor to write letters. Mike had phoned Nancy Garrity to drop by for a drink, but her phone hadn't answered.

The piped-in music, coming uninvited and water-bubbly from somewhere between Phil's and Mike's twin beds, was going strong with Rudolph Friml. They had called both the desk and Room Service about it, and had been told a maintenance man would be up presently to shut it off.

"I'll go along with you, Phil, because I respect you," Mike confided. "But I want to write something on the record. I think you're doing the wrong thing."

"We'll go into all that later. Let's go see them now."

"You go see them, and deliver my blessings."

Phil stood. "They're waiting for you, too."

"They're waiting for you, *mon capitaine*," Mike attested. "I'm going to stay right where I am, glued in my yellow shorts to this chair, and help finish this expensive gin. There's nothing in my contract that says I have to simper in front of the lady from the *Times*. Go well, Umfandi."

"There are rumors," said a reporter named Brooks, "that you expect, Dr. Morrow, to change the entire structure of the Alders Survey."

"I've heard those rumors," Phil conceded in the suite's living room, leaning against a couch arm and crossing his ankles, "and they are wrong and they are right, as most good rumors are. Our survey will essentially remain the same. We will continue to go from one city to another and to set up temporary offices. With the full cooperation of civic leaders and the volunteering of citizens of each town and city, we will strive to learn the sex conduct of the American people. We will continue to do so."

"But what about the difference? How will you differ from Dr. Alders?"

"I wouldn't call it a difference so much as a natural amplification of the original premise. When our team asks a question about sex, we won't scratch yeses and noes on the pads and turn our eyes away. We will pursue. We will draw out, invite subjects to talk, recommend treatment if it's indicated."

"Based on what authority?"

"Based on the fact that we are equipped professionally to listen, that Dr. Crayne and I are psychotherapists as well as psychologists and interviewers, and that we are able to deal with patients."

"Patients, sir?" snapped a reporter named Langhorne.

"All right, interviewees. Patients, if they give evidence of being potential patients. Everything, of course, will be in strictest confidence, as it's always been."

The reporter named Ames asked, "Did Dr. Alders accept or reject this method of interviewing?"

"He apparently accepted it. I am in charge of the Alders Institute Survey on Sex Conduct."

It was not the right way to answer, he judged, as he saw a few pairs of eyebrows raise.

"Shall we print the quote that way, Doctor?" Ames needled.

"Look," Phil said, addressing them all, intent on keeping his temper, "there's no need for any of us to spar here today. You want to know how many mistakes we're going to make in the survey before things roll smoothly. All right, let me assure you there will be some, but let me also assure you the mistakes will not be major ones. There shouldn't be any questions about our credentials. You might check Dr. Crayne and me with The American

Psychological Association. Dr. Crayne was associated with the Yalebrough Clinic for several years before he came to us. His excellent record there is available to any of you for a telephone call. Dr. Alders differed in certain respects with my theory of interviewing, but I think you, Mr. Ames, know in particular that Dr. Alders gave me the complete go-ahead some months ago. You read his comments in *Time, Newsweek,* and, if I remember correctly, in your own magazine, *Drake's.* If we're still a little suspect, may I recommend four or five scientific journals where my ideas were discussed, with basically unqualified acceptance, by Dr. Alders? I can supply these journals for you by the end of the day."

The conference took another half-hour, but the air was tolerably cleared. He knew he could have handled it infinitely better if he hadn't let them throw him on the defensive at the outset and, while the majority of the reporters seemed to be on his side by the time they were ready to leave, he wished he could've kept the tell-tale testiness out of his voice.

Dr. Rothschild gave him more lumps at dinner. "Vic Alders had a tremendous respect for you, Morrow, even when he thought you were going like a wild-eyed radical. His respect and affection for you were enough for me. I read the paper you did for the Von Oelrich crowd, and his dissenting footnotes along with it. It was a brilliant paper."

"Thank you," Phil began. "That was—"

"Thank me for nothing. I agreed with Alders' dissents. I don't think he went far enough in his dissents. I think he should've locked you in a closet and hidden your typewriter."

Phil sensed the man wasn't baiting him the way the reporters had, but he frowned and discovered himself on the defensive again. "For a man who's taking Dr. Alders' place legitimately, sir, I don't like hearing twice in the same day that I'm not authorized to take it."

Rothschild had no intention of being stared down. "You're going to hear it a thousand times more, my friend, before you turn the project into either a success or a fizzle. Why get this upset this early?"

"For a sound enough reason. You know how much I admire you and your work, Doctor, so you'll allow me to say what I'm going to say. I could've hired market researchers to snoop and poll around to see how popular I was with both the Rothschilds and the women's magazine ladies with their flower hats. I could've waited five or six months to see if everybody loves me, but by then valuable time and prestige—yes, the project's prestige—would be lost. If I'm any kind of professional, my job is to take the reins as my immediate superior handed them to me, and not wait around to see how many marriage proposals I get."

He paused for Rothschild to pull lightning from the heavens, but the older man merely sat back in the restaurant booth and stirred his coffee. "Dr. Alders was a responsible man," Phil went on. "The project was his whole life. It took him nearly twenty years to make everyone see he had great contributions to offer, that he wasn't just a meddlesome, anti-Victorian old pornographer. Why would he turn the Alders name over to a dub? Are people suspicious because I look as though I just entered high school? I'm aware of how I look."

"Drop that obvious red herring," Rothschild scolded. "People—and I'm people, too—are wary of you, not suspicious. We know how gifted you are. We're wary because you want to bite off more than a Freud would dare to chew. Alders' task was to gather sex data. You're not satisfied. You want to treat while you're gathering that data."

" 'Satisfied!' " Phil snorted. "Don't tell me *you* want scientists to be satisfied, too. Pasteur and Einstein and Freud and Jenner were advised to be satisfied with the status quo, too, weren't they? And you could help me with a hundred more names through history. You'll excuse me again, Dr. Roths-child, but what is this 'satisfied' talk? I always thought professional men considered that a filthy word."

"Just quiet down, you young pup," Rothschild said softly.

"I didn't mean to—"

"I said quiet down. You've yet to learn a quarter of all the medicine, psychology, psychiatry and overall pathology that I've forgotten, so don't give me snotty lectures about professional men. I submit that, for all your laudable ambition, your plan has one essential flaw. Analysis and therapy take as long as they do before a patient can realize a going equillibrium because of a stubborn little bastard called the unconscious. Until something else comes along—and it probably will be drugs—treatment won't and certainly shouldn't be shortened to the length of a handful of sessions. It was the very first psychiatrist, conceivably, who said, 'Rome wasn't built in a day.'

"I'll tell you why dissatisfaction can sometimes be very wrong, Morrow," Rothschild continued. "You want to help people live more useful and more healthful lives, and to that extent the best scientists who ever lived will applaud you. They'll even give you the benefit of the doubt and concede that what you're setting out to do will be of help, large or small, to ninety-seven per cent of the human beings you meet. But then you're guaranteed to run directly up against that other three per cent, the suggestibles. The latent homosexuals, the dormant lesbians, the not-quite sodomists. The churchly couples itching to commit adultery. Full-term treatment won't promise itself healthy results in all cases, but it has time enough to not only dissuade these people but to show them, according to their own terms of maturity, why they should dissuade themselves."

"Maybe you misread my paper, Doctor. I'm not inviting moral lawlessness. Mike Crayne and I know latents when we meet them. The paper at Von Oelrich specifically stated that when sexual trouble is brewing, and when the interviewee knows it's brewing but doesn't have ego or information enough to cope with it on an adult basis, we recommend professional help. And we go farther than that. If treatment isn't available within the immediate community, we find out where it is available."

"That, of itself, is hunky-dory. But you also intend to take it on yourselves to treat, over a period of each short stop at each city, those 'patients' you believe to be neither emotionally sick nor emotionally well. Did I misread that passage?"

"I didn't use the word 'treat'," Phil admitted, "But in the long run that's the word I meant, based purely on feeling out and the eventual access of a team of graduate psychotherapists."

"You're in for a peck of trouble, my friend," Dr. Rothschild said as he nodded to the waiter for the check, "even if you have more luck with your experiment than I think you'll have. As I say, I'll spot you ninety-seven per cent of your clients as successes, and anyone will tell you that as a good doctor, I'm a lousy gambler. It's that three per cent you and your coterie have to worry about."

"Three per cent out of a hundred per cent..."

Rothschild bit off the tip of a cigar and nodded. "Three per cent," he repeated and his smile was not a friendly smile. "You're about to find, Dr. Morrow, that three per cent makes up a lot of people. Unhappy people, troubled people, maybe even disturbed people. In the course of ten days, over an eight or ten hour optimum each, what safeguards do you have in your 'science' to guarantee that John Doe won't be stimulated to masturbate, to go to bed with his neighbor's wife, or to murder his own wife?"

The remainder of the stay in the off-route city was hurried. Mrs. Alders served Phil a tall glass of ginger ale with a weak shot of rye, and followed it up with endless cups of tea and reminiscenses about Victor. Victor had mowed the russet, carpety backyard lawn on every Saturday morning he was at home. Here were the walls he'd painted, and there was the untuned grand piano on which he'd one-fingered his way through all of Bach. The Bach sheet music hadn't been removed from the stand after months only because none of the other Alders knew how to play.

At no time through that evening did Mrs. Alders ask what right Phil Morrow had to take over the Alders Institute Survey. Her husband had written or said that Philip argued incessantly but that he was the natural heir to the project. She was alarmed to hear that he owned neither hat nor scarf, even in winter, and sermonized over him about the pit-falls of naked pores and the ills they could produce. He promised to buy a hat and scarf.

The Alders' children, three daughters and a son, none under thirty years old, were married, lived outside the state, and were engaged in work wholly separate from sex-history compilation. The daughters were mothers and PTA leaders. The son was a dentist in Louisville, Kentucky. They appeared to have no interest in their father other than as a father. They were eager to get back to their homes.

On the flight east, Phil again studied the reports on Waymouth, New York, sent him by Herb Graham. The civic groups there wouldn't turn out at the airport with their brass bands, Herb had observed, but there were no evidences of premature opposition, either. Reading over the regimen Dr. Alders had prepared, Phil rather wished the team could have tried out its new legs in a less challenging setting.

They had never visited a suburban community *as* a suburban community before. The Doctor himself had chosen Waymouth, twenty-three miles from Grand Central Station in Manhattan, as an ideal setting for a fair sampling of the sex behavior of emigrated urbanites. The town, although it was one of the oldest in the state, had had a vigorous rebirth shortly after the end of World War II, when an influx of well-to-do families had preceded new businesses and factories. "Let's see," Dr. Alders had said, "just how sexually tense an uprooted atmosphere can make people."

It had never been attempted before on Alders' face-to-face kind of survey basis. It was an ambitious and fine idea, Phil conceded, but it inherently provided its own brace of dangers. There was no legitimate way, certainly not at this late hour, to beg off for another month or so and interview a less potentially inflammable area.

In his seat near the plane's window, he covertly eyed the others. All in all, Mike Crayne couldn't be improved on, but the others bothered him. Nelson Partrige, the bachelor, was ingrown, possibly just a trace effeminate, and hardly the most stable man Phil had met. Nancy Garrity, though workmanlike and decidedly adequate on the job, bothered him even more, for no instantly discernible reason. Dr. Alders had chosen her because Ian Garrity, her father and his colleague, had recommended her, and maybe that should have been good enough for Phil because the Doctor would never have taken psychologists on unless he was convinced they were professionally competent.

Phil knew he would have to evaluate his feelings about Nancy carefully; he suspected that she disturbed him solely because she was a woman doing a man's work and that sort of behavior had always made him angry. Still, she looked like no other psychologist who had ever lived. She was in her twenties and extremely pretty. Her hair was burnished, her occasionally tight clothes were implicative, and her molded breasts were often much too clearly defined for comfort. So far as he knew, nothing occupied her outside of her job, no husband or sweetheart, and he wondered if her deliberate singlemindedness was altogether healthy. She could volunteer the most intimate descriptions of sex relations among her interviewees without batting an evil or embarrassed eye and, while this spoke excellently for her as a researcher, there seemed something odd about a healthy young woman being so incredibly unaffected by what she roused and recorded.

She sat on the other side of the aisle now, immersed in the notebooks preparatory to Waymouth, and he would have forfeited a night's coveted sleep to learn whether or not she knew her skirt was rucked back as imprudently as it was.

"The chief test of determining if a man is great lies in his sense of humor or lack of it," Mike was saying, slouching next to Phil. "True?"

"Okay. Who's testing whom?"

"I'm testing you, my leader. Here's a line in Earl Wilson's column: 'As the Alders surveyer said to the sex maniac, "You're okay in my book, boy".' "

Phil grinned and nodded. "That's funny. Am I great now?"

"Immortal," Mike yawned, and slouched deeper in his seat to doze.

The stewardess came with coffee and tea orders. Phil smiled, shook his head, and looked away. The picture of Rothschild returned, and so did the recollection of the man's baiting about the ninety-seven per cent of any given community.

"It's that three per cent you and your coterie have to worry about," Rothschild had said.

He wondered about what he and the others would find in Waymouth.

CHAPTER TWO

✤ ✤ ✤

I N THE middle of the town, the hands of the clock in front of the ancient courthouse waited at half-past ten. Within an hour most of the Waymouth residents would be getting ready for bed, after the eleven o'clock news and the final beer or iced tea (or, in the newer Underwood section, the final Scotch and water).

Griffin Street, the town's main thoroughfare, was lit up brightly at this time of night, but it was nearly deserted. A visitor, having heard of Waymouth—reborn in 1946 and grown since as the shining symbol of suburbia, with its vivid images of high sophistication, continuous cocktail parties and blithe adulteries—would, at first inspection, ask what joker had invented the image; except for a few centers of activity, in the remoter neighborhoods, Waymouth appeared to set its alarm and be asleep before the Late Show's third commercial.

On this particular summer night, a week before the Alders Institute Survey on Sex Conduct was to arrive for fourteen days of intensive interviewing, a girl and a young man walked, their arms linked, in the direction of Bridgewell Park. They had taken as much care as they could not to be seen, for a man and woman who entered Bridgewell Park after dark were immediately suspect. Neither could afford gossip. They had announced their engagement the Sunday before, and the suaver citizens in Underwood would have judged the after-dark ban as a tiresome holdover from the Nineteenth Century. But Sally Warner and Bob Raymond did not move in Underwood circles.

"Your hand is like ice," Bob said.

"Who asked you?" she objected good-naturedly, unused to what they were on their way to do, nervous and just a little frightened, wishing they could be more spontaneous in their talk and movements than they obviously were.

In sharp contrast to the brightness of Griffin Street, the shadows from the tight row of houses on one side of the street and the high stone wall and trees on the opposite side gave the walk an unbroken deepening cast. The wall, beside which the couple moved, extended for several blocks and served to cage in the Park, Waymouth's chief landmark. By day, it was a park dedicated to summer outings, picnics, holiday speeches and ceremonies. Children loved to run in the upper field and to wade in its brook. The beginning of Bridgewell Park was innocent enough, with its publicly donated statue of Civil War General Hamilton Sherwood standing next to a cannon and a neatly arranged pyramid of cannon balls. Off to one side sat the headstones of twelve Civil War veterans. Later on there were swings and benches.

"Well, we're here."

Sally frowned. "No, let's keep walking. I'd die if anyone saw us."

While the beginning of Bridgewell Park ran parallel to Griffin Street and thus close to civilization, even though divided by the wall, the path veered sharply and then gradually led into the heart of the park, considerably cut off from the main arteries of social contact. At night, empty of children and speechmakers and strollers, the place was secret and foreboding.

By now the half-moon was brighter and the night darker. The young couple had already passed the sharp turn and, walking in shadow, mounted a slight incline. They selected a bench, set back but facing the direction from which they had come. To the back of them lay a narrow footpath, better noticed by day and used by the children as a short cut back to the main entrance.

Once the couple seated themselves, the trees and bushes seemed crowded in around them and gave them the feeling of complete seclusion and secret invasion. Only a soft breeze disturbed the leaves with a sighing restlessness.

But, aside from this, the park was deathly quiet.

"You know," Bob Raymond offered, sitting erect and uncomfortable, like a self-conscious poser for a complicated camera, "when Mother and I moved here last year, we lived right over there on Orange. I could look out my bedroom window and see this very bench."

Her instinctive stiffness made it clear he shouldn't have mentioned his mother. Mrs. Raymond was still fighting their engagement as venomously as possible. Bob taught mechanical drawing at Waymouth High in the Arborston district and he had built a good name for himself in his one term of teaching. The mother had desperately fought his getting involved with this girl, this daughter of a department-store janitor.

"I'm sorry," he said hastily. "Tonight Mother is out of bounds, I promise. Along with taxes, land crabs, and all other disturbers of the peace."

"Please, Bob. Don't make me think of myself as something from under a rock, out to snatch you away from anyone. If there was any way I could make your mother accept me—

"It's my fault. I just shouldn't have brought up the subject. There's plenty of time for that, anyway."

His arms went out to her and she knew, finally, that her safe old bag of tricks, complete with coyness, gentle teasing and reasonable fear, had emptied. They had spent hours together yesterday and this afternoon, talking out her reasons for wanting to wait until they were married before she gave herself to him. There had been rocky moments, scraping along the edges of sarcasm and argument, and she had come to agree that her long-held set of reasons for waiting were pompous, unrealistic, even juvenile. She would be his wife soon and she loved him. The romantically agonizing holding off had made perfect sense back in—well, away back in her own dark ages. It was ridiculous now.

For a moment he looked at her, as he brought her to him, with a lover's pure uncritical delight. He lightly touched the smoky shadows of her hair and her white throat, and her worried happiness glowed through her skin and smouldered in bright darkness from her eyes. She had a delicate, almost oval face, childlike in its seeming incorruptibility. His hand lowered to her breast and she strove to assure herself that she was happy, that all of this was right, that her training had beem musty and Victorian, that lovers could indeed love without the shackling of guilt if trust was real and meaningful. His hand cupped the breast and squeezed it, and Sally, awakening, brought his other hand to her knee. His body moved forward slightly as he worked the hem of the skirt back and slid his damp palm over her thigh.

When she raised her head to meet his lips, she saw the other person standing on the bank, within the clump of half-dead bushes in back of the bench. Her hand darted away from his face and she gasped.

"What's wrong Sally?"

"Be—behind you…"

A tall man stood on the bank, his huge hands hanging limp at his sides. His attention was focused squarely on her, as though Bob did not exist.

Sally had jerked back but now she sat immobile, her eyes wide in waiting. The frightened Bob rose swiftly from the bench and retreated a step or two, as if to cloak himself in darkness. The stranger was not a man but a boy, probably not more than seventeen or eighteen. His angry face shone with the aid of a meager beam of color from a distant light-post. His shirt was open at the neck and his blue jeans were caked with dirt. Everything about him appeared huge in the light: his broad chest, the arms, the hands—especially the hands.

Bob started to say something and to move away, but the rustle of huge feet, stepping out of the bushes, stopped him. Even before he felt the hand on the back of his neck, he emitted a whimper of pain and fear.

The boy gripped his big hands into Bob's arms and yanked him around. He held the arms tight and shoved him back so that the beam of light now shone brightly on them both. Furiously he threw Bob to the hard earth and brought a heavy shoe down on his face. He raised the foot and kicked the contorted face, over and over again, increasing his strength. Sally grabbed at the boy, struggling to form words to plead, but she could not halt him. He kicked and ground his foot into the face until the face and neck were a great mass of blood.

The boy pulled him up by the hair and dragged him to one of the gravestones which lay a few feet away from the bench. The enormous hands pushed the blond head down to hit the stone. There was the sickening sound of a sharp crack.

Sally ran.

She did not know whether she had screamed, whether she was screaming now, whether terror had made her mute. Retreating, she bumped into a tree. She wheeled, still able to hear the heavy breathing and choked curses. She ran, into the inky depths of the park.

Numbing streaks of ice flushed through her as she ran. *They mustn't find me. Nobody. Nobody must see me here. God o God get me out of here don't let anyone see me.*

Still the hushed sounds of violence followed her. She tried to find the path, any path, that would free her. The night had become so dismally dark and she sent up formless prayers that she be saved, that she escape this maze of bushes and tombstones and trees she knew so well.

But where? Where was it? Where was anything she could recognize? Where were the swings and seesaws and picnic tables?

Don't let me get lost! she called to her jiffy-service God, *don't let anyone know I was here! O God save me don't let anyone—*

She tripped and fell over one of the rotting benches. Her breast struck again the half-wood, half-iron; the pain merged keenly with a savage pleasure that told her she wasn't dead, that she still was alive because she could feel pain. She worked to force herself up from the concrete path *(I've found a path, I'm not lost)* but all strength drained from her and watery paralysis set into her legs.

Rest. Rest for just one second. She couldn't hear the sounds any more; that was good. It was dark, he wouldn't be able to find her, no one would see her here in the park. She attempted to breathe in some controlled order. The pain at her breast deepened and she was convinced she was bleeding. The picture of Bob Raymond sped past, of Bob defending himself. He was dead. No one could blame her for anything.

The shock of selfishness overwhelmed her, but she did not concentrate on that now. She pushed her palms flat against the bench seat and started to rise, but she found herself falling again. She reached for one of the Civil War veterans' grave markers which dotted the park's lawn and she wept frustration and giddiness and exhaustion. The throbbing at her breast was sensual in its pain.

Soon she was sure she could not move, that she never would move again, that she was going to faint.

She thought she could hear a vague rustling. She looked up and saw him standing in front of her, his powerful hands once more limp at his sides.

"No..." she breathed stertorously, certain he could not hear her.

Her senses filmed an instant or an eternity after she felt him grab at her skirt, and the dream shadow which preceded the moment of awakening flickered over her face. She drifted over enormous chasms of space. The hard outline of night softened.

The light filtering through the long trees was dimmed by the thickness of the park's growth.

At twenty minutes before noon, three days later, Marianne Sherwood came up out of a druggedly deep sleep in the house she despised. Lately, consciousness of the Evers Drive house took instantaneous precedence over everything else as soon as she wakened, and set a tone which promised depression. She had dealt with it more and more over the past halfyear with a medicinal belt of vodka before coffee, but she had made a solemn Vow to drink, before the morning coffee, only in extra special emergencies.

At an extremely attractive and willowy thirty-five, she had been everywhere she'd wanted to go, had met too many people to be outraged or particularly surprised by much of anything, and she liked to think of herself as being utterly without superstition. But the sauce, she had discovered, was first cousin to a transient lover. It could be counted on to perform the vital chores at night with glowing success; in the grim grip of morning, it was an eventual son of a bitch, as trustworthy as a boy pyrhana.

No vodka this morning, she decided. I'll find a way to bear this detestable house with its shades full of mournful mystery. I have some things riding for me, haven't I? Yes, somewhere around. In this treacherous house, living with a husband as restless as I, surviving in this Godawful hick town, there are still points of current interest to bring me out of this bed this week.

There is the Sally Warner story—and that sourball of a maid will forget again, naturally, to bring the newspaper to the breakfast table. There is Dan Parrish, who has begun to court me again in earnest, with all the confidence on land, sea and foam that he is once more about to bowl one grand strike with me—and who can tell? Maybe he just might, at that.

Of course he might. He will.

There is the Alders sex thing. The survey chugging its way to Waymouth, with pipe-smoking young scholars in button-down blue shirts eager to record just how layable we so-called suburban matrons are. Come one, come all to the greatest show in Waymouth.

There is Aaron Miles. And Aaron Miles supercedes all the rest.

Marianne Sherwood slid her long, smooth legs over the side of the double bed on this Saturday summer morning, determined not to give in to the hangover she surmised was about to do its best to be a dilly.

She had drunk a great quantity of vodka last night, more than usual—she would make a point of deciphering the reason later, after everything else had been attended to—but she had begun to teach herself the maxim that hangovers will regretfully steal away if you simply move to ignore them. She had introduced herself to hard, serious yet wholly discreet drinking ten or more years ago, and she had had her share of the morning-after miseries. But drinking had not lessened her, as it had depleted her mother and her rat packs of stepfathers. She had a bear's appetite and in company she never got sodden or hysterical or perceptibly bitchy or noticeably sick. Her complexion and her legs were as perfect as they always had been. She was still a flawless 36-24-36 despite the vats of both good and bad booze, and there was no vindictive swami in the neighborhood to tell her in the ominous voice she used to hear that she wouldn't go on that way for the next thousand and a half years.

The bathroom mirror this morning had a momentarily different report for her, but she had learned to roll with that punch, too. The slate-colored eyes were dull and the whites were bloodshot. The untouched blonde hair was a field of trampled wheat. But Murine and a comb would race those problems out to sea, and toast and eggs and coffee would, in another half-hour, make her ready to beat Marciano. Was there another Waymouth haus-frau who could make a like boast?

A long, soapy shower eased most of the woes, and she stepped out to dry herself with a mammoth Turkish towel. Not bad, the full-length mirror told her, not bad at all; you won't have to apologize for that shape, ma'am, for a long, long time. She kneaded lots of cologne into her body and dressed hurriedly, without under-clothes, in tailored plaid slacks and one of her husband Steve's shaggy sport shirts. Steve's shaggy sport shirts, she repeated, feeling a marvelous upbeat of energy and self-assurance. I must remember to see if I can say that the next time I'm plastered.

She dug her small feet into her good-luck huraches, the ones she'd worn during the Mexico location shooting with Gregory Peck, and, lighting her first cigarette for the day, went down the wide stairs.

The town wore late August like a merciless flannel. The day was bright, but a silky haze seemed to hang over the town. Marianne strode past the housekeeper in the downstairs hall-way of the old, hateful house—Mrs. Quigley had worked for the Sherwoods since shortly before the War of 1812; the two women had taken an instant dislike to one another when Marianne had moved in as a bride six years ago and both had silently agreed from the beginning to converse only when absolutely necessary—out onto the patio. Sure enough, both papers were there. *The New York Times* and The *Waymouth Spectator.* I will have to wait for that lousy maid, she thought, and genuflect with apologies.

The old but Scotch-taped Sherwood house in Underwood sat at the very top of Waymouth and looked down over most of the burgeoning New York suburb. From the west, one could see the heavily commercialized shopping centers, jampacked with the Manhattan department-store branches which had done so much to help kill sales at Sherwood's.

From the east, if one ever bothered any longer to look, one could see at least half of Northrop Avenue, the first street built in

Waymouth, which meant that it had been built over a hundred years ago.

Marianne paused to regard for a moment, as she nearly always did on summer mornings, Northrop Avenue. The avenue, bordered by walnut trees, was disproportionately wide, its solemn, unbroken sweep extending to a distant rectangular arch, gleaming in the sunlight under which it passed.

That's Julia Havilland's street, Marianne thought with a smile she did not bother to contain. And oh, boy, just try to imagine what goosed-up sparks would fly if the gents from the Alders sex patrol located Julia and asked to interview her! I can see the marquee now. Dracula Meets The Virgin Queen. Al Capone Dates Alice in Wonderland.

That's my mission for the day, and in spades. I will telephone Julia Havilland and needle the frostbitten hell out of her. If she's never been on anyone else's couch but her old bore of a husband's, I'll see that she gets on Alders'.

Waiting for breakfast, Marianne helped herself to the Silex and thumbed through *The Times* till she reached the drama section. As expected, they had a complete enough coverage of Aaron Miles' trip to Manhattan. The eccentric but incontestable titan of Hollywood, the five-foot-one Goliath among producer-directors who had taken the mantle of Cecil B. De-Mille would be in the city within a few days for a first of three visits to confer with Dayne Pictures on his next Biblical epic, *Lot's Wife*. He would, of course, stay at the Plaza, He would, of course, have his army of fifteen aides-de-Miles with him.

And he would, of course, be only too happy to see Marianne Terrin. ("You might just not remember me, Mr. Miles, with all you have to do." "Ah, Miss Terrin, how gratifying. Bless you. How nice of you to call a weary old man." "I was the slave girl in *Sons of Solomon*. I had that hair-pulling scene with Susan Hayward." "Dont' feel you have to remind me, my dear. My memory is impeccable, and so are you. Would you be free for lunch this afternoon? I haven't yet finished casting the role of—")

A few days, she thought. He's impossible to get to in Hollywood, but New York is just an outlying district of Keokuk and Madison. He'll see me. Why in the hell wouldn't he?

And that, she sensed eagerly, will be that, kind hearts. I will be put on *Lot's Wife*—he's sending all these phony feelers cross country about hiring Elizabeth Taylor but she's guaranteed to turn him down—and I will say an unembittered goodbye to this freaky little town just twenty-three miles from the city, and to clammy friend husband who doesn't want a wife nearly so much as he wants a mommy, and to clammy friend father-in-law who holds the purse strings so tightly that I'm not guaranteed of a thin quarter, and to all the other clammy friends who go with the shooting match.

Eunice appeared on the patio with a tray full of breakfast and nodded. Marianne nodded back, not looking up entirely; Eunice was a road show Mrs. Quigley and it had been made clear that love was not precisely the magic word in this house.

"Oh—uh, Mr. Sherwood left you a—uh—message before he went to work this morning," Eunice informed, eyes deep in the scrambled eggs. "He's got this full-day conference going for him and he don't think he'll be home much before midnight."

"Thank you, Eunice," Marianne answered drily.

"Welcome," Eunice said and trudged away.

Full-day conference, my wounded grandmother, Marianne thought, only fleetingly perturbed. The last time he had a full-day conference, that aging playboy husband of mine with the beginnings of a belly paunch, was when he talked Sally Warner or one of her slutty cohorts from the store to take off for a weekend at Bear Mountain or the Hamptons.

Funny, she decided, putting Sally Warner, the rapist's celebrity, into the hopper with the batch of other hopeful conquests of Steve's. I have no assurance, not even a hint, that she plays around, either with him or any other man. Good God, am I turning into one of those abysmal Waymouth crones who lap up this guilt-by-association bit? A pretty, well-built, outgoing twenty-one-year-old unmarried salesgirl at Sherwood's Department Store is involved in a rape, and all of a nasty sudden there is a tacit, tooth-clucking understanding that she had led the rapist on. That's the poop making the shopping center and tea room rounds.

And I, the original sin forgiver, am unconsciously joining the hen brigades.

She was surprised to find, opposite the drama page, that *The Times* was still covering the Sally Warner case. But then, why not? It wasn't only a local tragedy. Most newspapers in the country, very likely, were still referring to it.

The Times gave it only a few pithy paragraphs but, as was to be expected, told all there was to know to date. The rapist-killer, nineteen, Vincente Polumbo, mentally retarded, a ward of the Father Chalmers Home three miles outside Waymouth, had been found late Friday night in the vicinity of the Home with the victim Robert Raymond's wallet in his hand. He had confessed everything, calmly. "I like everybody at the Home," the youth told police, "and I needed money to buy them all presents." He was being observed by a group of psychiatrists. The Warner girl was still in semi-shock at Waymouth General Hospital and doctors were concerned.

God, thought Marianne, the poor girl. Rape or pretended rape, what's the difference? No one should ever have to go through something like that. I, with all my ready answers, I would have stayed in their aptly phrased semi-shock not for four days but till the return of the Ice Age.

Why can't I bring myself to get off my fancy can and go to her? I don't know her except for recognizing her now and then at her post at the store's perfume counter, and she surely doesn't know me (unless she's been bedding down with Steve, and I, in my rampant, stagey Christianity, am not prepared to make any melodramatic charges), but what does that matter? The rest of the local gossip goes that she has two people in her life, and both of them are far-out odd balls. Her father, the store's night watchman, is a crusty old devil of a widower who watches the night and sings hoarse psalms in favor of everlasting virginity. And her old sister, the gas company cashier, the professional spinster who is the wholesome embodiment of Pap's teachings.

I should go over to that antiseptic-happy hospital and take some flowers or a bottle of gin, if only to show one woman that another woman is available with love.

But I won't.

I'll write her a nice letter from Dayne Studios in Culver City, California.

There was every good indication, according to this week's *Variety,* that Charlton Heston was going to play the male lead in *Lot's Wife.* Now *there* would be a feather!

Marianne Sherwood finished her breakfast and carried her cup of coffee into the warehouse of a living room, with all its effects decorated in Early Eyesore, the room she abhorred most of all.

The whole house had been presented to her and Steve as a wedding gift when they'd returned from their honeymoon in San Francisco. "My children," Lawrence J. Sherwood had sanctimoniously intoned, placing his withered fingers on her and the obsequious Steve's shoulders, "I can imagine nothing which would give me deeper pleasure than to offer you this, the Sherwood house. It has withstood fire, flood, famine, and Franklin D. It will last forever, which portends well for your union."

The Silas Marner of an old bastard always talked like that, as if he were addressing a joint session of Congress.

It was a miserable house, and the roof leaked.

The idea occurred to her again to phone Julia Havilland, down on Northrop Avenue. She had wondered about lean but well-formed, scaredy-cat Julia from the time she'd met her at that first loathsome civic betterment meeting, in the grammar-school basement where each leather seat cushion was secretly made of marble. Julia, whose husband was the most razzmatazz realtor of the century, was in charge of everything conceivably Waymouth, from demanding better lunches for students to painting public johns. She had been so industriously sexless while remaining so basically sexual that she had caught Marianne's eye, and here and there they had had a few words together. I'm just being bitchy again, she thought now; her business is her business and my business is my business. Why do I get such a boot out of making her feel so obviously embarrassed when I say hello to her?

Honest, Judge, I never once snipped off a live butterfly's wings. Lay off.

She had just found Julia's number in the red address book and had reached for the receiver, when the telephone rang. She answered it immediately.

"There's this remarkable football game being played this afternoon near the Guggenheim Museum," said Dan Parrish. "You come into town and see it with me. I have ringside seats right on the—whatever they call it—the diamond."

"You never saw a football game in your depraved life."

"As a matter of fact—"

"As a matter of double fact, I've never been to the Guggenheim. I'm ashamed to admit it."

"Meet me at the Algonk Bar at two. We'll just make it."

"You're rushing the lady."

"Two o'clock. It's on Forty-fourth Street. Any cab will find it."

Marianne agreed, replaced the receiver, and hurried back upstairs. She stripped in haste. She selected the flimsiest bra and scantiest panties she owned. The white-silk buttoned blouse came next. Then she picked a frivolous candy-stripe jumper (*If he makes any obstreperous gaos about jumpers, I'll shoot him for an obvious lout; lovingly, but I'll shoot him).* She swung gaily back and forth at her reflection in the full-length mirror, adjusting the wide tan belt, and would have laid a bet that he would approve of the sight. She ran the comb through her long yellow hair once more, made sure of the diaphragm, and left the house. She drove the Thunderbird to the train station with minutes to spare, and rode the 1:17 to New York.

He was waiting for her at the bar, patiently strumming the stem of his glass. Dan Parrish wasn't so handsome in person as he invariably was when she wasn't with him, but today she felt no minor disappointment as she had felt once or twice before. She would have preferred him without the mustache, and she had told him as much, but that was mere carping; this was no time to look a gift man in the mustache.

"The Guggenheim probably isn't even open," he remarked during their second round of Gibsons.

"I own a ouija board that warned me you were going to say that, and in those same words, and at this point in time."

"Then what are we doing here?"

"I stand corrected as always," Marianne replied, "but I believe we're having a drink."

"That's no excuse," he said. "I have drinks down at my plantation, too, and at about one-eighth of the cost here."

"Awright, awready. You're pulling my leg or twisting my arm, or some damn contortion."

"Well, which? One is a temptation, the other is a drag."

Marianne nodded and drained her drink. "I never understood modern art, anyway. I never even understood the frames on them."

By now, her third visit to his apartment house off Mitchell Place, the antique elevator operator didn't bother to raise those preacher's white eyebrows. In the apartment, she made every casual effort to draw him into conversations about Majorca, Hollywood, television, Rilke, and whether there truly was a

Guggenheim Museum. The talk was surface and scarcely necessary. The drinks were barely poured when the virtuous blouse, the wide tan belt, and the jumper had been flung to parts unknown.

"You certainly are an eager, how they say, beaver," she stated as he guided her to his bedroom.

"And you certainly don't put up much of an argument in the, how they say, clinches."

"Would you like me more if I did?"

He looked at her for, she was certain, the very first time since she'd met him. "How they say, indeed? Repeat that, please, for the latecomers."

"Would you like me more if I did?"

"Will you kindly tell me what liking has to do with what we're heading toward the process of doing?"

"I talk too much?"

"You talk far too much."

"But you'll just maybe like me when I'm old and gray?"

"Ask me again when you're old and gray. Right now, get the hell where you belong. We have important work to do."

"Yowzah, kind master."

Julia Havilland awoke from a dream. She lay still, hoping her immobility would hold the dream as the spirit of a dream sometimes is captured and held in a statue. She had been with Erik. He had bent over her, taken her in his arms, and kissed her. His love had filled her so completely that the intensity had wakened her.

But her dream was not to be held as in a statue. The mold was volatile, and despair flowed over her in familiar, surfless, soundless waves.

The dream shamed her and she got out of bed swiftly, almost as if the bed itself were responsible for giving her the thoughts she knew she should not have had. She held off for a moment before regarding Charles in the other twin bed, aware in her painful embarrassment that it was absolute craziness to imagine he knew what she had dreamed; she had always risen earlier than Charles, the same good, kind man who strangely irritated her at parties when he loudly announced to guests that he slept like an infant, that he fell asleep the second his head hit the pillow, that he required an alarm clock *and* Julia to rouse him in the morning.

Charles wasn't in his bed now when she looked, and she remembered that she had excused herself from the back porch at around noon, complaining of a headache, and had come up here to take one of her infrequent afternoon naps. Brushing her rawly damp palms down over her hips, she realized for the first time that she had simply stripped before getting into her bed, rather than bother to fiddle with the air conditioner, but that she was naked. The nakedness, coupled with the vivid memory of the dreadful, distressing dream, shook her and she hurried for her clothes. The second-floor bedroom windows were opened. The afternoon sun shone strangely and sent beams of milky light out over the lawn below.

Only when she had begun to calm did the thought occur to her that her flushed anxiety was wholly unwarranted, that any sensible person—meaning Julia Havilland—could tell her it was nothing more than a minor betrayal of her tendency to be a trifle melodramatic. I am a grown, quite mature woman of thirty-eight, she reminded herself, of better than average intelligence and sensitivities. I am attractive enough for most normal purposes and, in spite of myself, I command considerable respect in my community. At points of crisis I have stood up against the entire city council. What is there in a silly dream, a very temporary retreat to the adolescent wastelands, to hurt me?

Once assured, and stretching her body to its imposingly full height, she finished dressing, scissored long fingers through lambent brown hair, snatched a single satisfied glance at herself in the bureau mirror, and descended the stairs to find Charles.

"Headache gone, dear?" he asked, partially looking up from his yellow legal pad. "You look better than I've ever seen you look."

"Aren't you the thoughtful one?" she said, pushing the screen door back and emerging onto the lawn. "The nap worked wonders. I can't even remember having the headache."

"Um," he nodded, and returned to his work.

The sleek, immaculately kept lawn was restful at this time of day, and she felt lucky to have Charles here, home with her, on a weekend afternoon, even if he did surround himself with work. He sat at the picnic table next to the hammock, adding up the columns of figures which represented the week's profit or loss in Waymouth real estate and insurance sales, a thick-set, irremediably balding man of fifty-one who had lost his good, fresh young looks over a gradual period of their years together, but who nevertheless was the man she loved. She sat beside him in the old but comfortable wicker chair and pretended to study the luxuriant rose garden in the direct center of the yard.

She had overheard the nasty, spiteful observations about her husband at the country club and at civic meetings, and she had been able to fill in for herself the atrocious details she had not heard. Charlie Havilland? Oh, a good enough guy and a demon when it comes to sales, but don't trust him personally for an instant away from the cash register, his formula-feeding symbol. A total and yawn-provoking square. Babbitt's reincarnation. The dullest thing to come out of Waymouth, New York, since phony soapsuds were invented.

And if you're not convinced, get a load of his missus. Charlie, the original pamphlet quoter, would be the first to grab your lapel and tell you a man in business can be judged by the woman he's married to. Enough said. You know she's a female only by the pink booties. Drab clothes. No expression on her face. Not enough makeup to bloat a moth. But all of it comes back to Charlie Havilland. You don't blame the wife, you blame Charlie.

Somebody had better wake him up and tell him President McKinley's dead. But the shock might be fatal.

It was cruel, unjustified talk. Julia could count at least a dozen important missions of hers in Waymouth. The most important of them all was to protect Charles from ever even sensing that the town he had been born in, brought up in and cherished had so little personal admiration for him. That was duty enough for any wife, and it was a holy duty.

"Headache gone, dear?" Charles repeated absently in a mumbling monotone as his busy eyes moved from the yellow pad to a sheaf of papers.

"Yes, dear. All gone."

"Good."

"Ah—you never did tell me whether you finally sold the Plotkin house," Julia inquired, reaching for threads.

"—have the peppers and eggs for lunch?"

"What?"

"Is Maude going to let us have the peppers and eggs for lunch?"

"Oh. Yes, dear," Julia replied. From the first day they had been able to afford a maid who could cook, eleven or twelve years ago, Charles had decided on a diet of peppers and eggs at each Saturday lunch he could find time to come home for. In all those years their Saturday lunches had consisted of peppers and eggs. She had never once suggested they have corned beef and eggs, or hash and eggs. There was no need.

Reclining in the wicker chair, Julia Havilland reached over to take *The Waymouth Spectator* and saw the by-now muddy photograph of Sally Warner, the one the paper had carried every day since the horrible assault and murder. She started to read the latest developments in the case, but discovered that the developments triggered a new recollection of her dream. The one of Erik, gleaming in his nakedness, bending over her and taking her. *And who, pray, is Erik? I never knew an Erik in my life!*

There had been these insolent dreams before, she thought, those dreams about sex, of her languishing on immense lounges and rising wantonly into powerful arms. For some perplexingly unknown reason, though, she had dreamed them only during daytime naps, never at night.

Why?

Did it have anything to do with Charles?

There had been sex with Charles once, only once, in the past two months, and then as something of an afterthought on his part. Fifty-one, according to all the fashionable charts and polls, was certainly still a period of physical competence, of potency. Charles, she recalled, had been fagged out at bedtime and eager for immediate sleep when he had been forty-one. It was a horrid and overly intimate thing to even think, but, she recognized, her disinterest in lovemaking had very possibly been instigated, unwittingly, by Charles.

Julia Havilland, who had been far too tall and far too slender from the time she had first been allowed to date, was not insensitive to the criticisms leveled against her as well as against Charles. She did dive into every betterment association the city developed, and very often agreed to lead it. She worked hard and long to put Waymouth over the top culturally, and there was no doubt that a handful of biddies mocked her seriousness, but what could she do except her best? She, like Charles, had been born in Waymouth. She loved the town, believed in it, wanted to see it thrive. "Security and an abiding sense of the decency in ourselves," she had heard herself say last month during one of the Way-mouth Ladies teas, "is all we and our community ask of one another." She had believed it then, and believed it still.

Without warning, though, two events had nastily invaded the proper calm of Waymouth since that tea to prove unsettling: the unpleasantness about the Warner girl and the announcement that those horrid Alders people were going to camp on this good city's unwelcoming doorstep to pry and nose their way into the privacy of the fives of the residents here, both decent and inde-cent citizens alike.

The Alders event was, of course, the more objectionable of the two. A saucy young girl who brazenly goes into Bridge-well Park after dark with a vigorous young man surely can't ever plead later that she hadn't been in the market for trouble. It was too bad, naturally, that young Raymond had been killed, but then what had stopped him from staying home where he obviously belonged? No, you could shed tears for them only up to a point. Violence visits most often when you open the door for it.

But no one—certainly, no one of breeding—should ever have opened the Waymouth door to the Alders researchers and their depraved kind; they fitted into the fabric of New York City, per-haps, but New York City, for all its closeness by train and car, was fundamentally a million miles from the propriety and gentle grace of Waymouth.

Julia did not want them here. She had led the fight against their being allowed in, over the super-sophisticated acceptance of, of all respectable people, Mayor Sandstrom, Edwin Powell from the City Council, and even Reverend Pendleton from the First Presbyterian Church. The loud, often shrill argument that the intended survey was totally serious and in the full interests of research had sounded like out-and-out balderdash to her and she had not been afraid to say so, even when her one good friend from *The Waymouth Spectator,* Geoffrey Wiswell, had come out editorially in favor of the community being spotlighted in the country's eyes as some morbid sort of sexual guinea pig.

The votes were in and, according to today's *Spectator* state-ment, the Alders' animalistic emissaries, Dr. Philip Morrow, Dr. Michael Crayne, Dr. Nelson Partridge, and Dr. Nancy Garrity *(that was impossible to fathom: a young lady of considerable back-ground and, as could be seen in the newspaper photograph, with an attractive face that showed decency and character, asking the most intimate questions of people!)* soon would make their deplorable invasion with their own brand of spears and lances. Already the lines of volunteers—and Julia knew some of them personally, had known some of them all her life—were truly remarkable.

"Wouldn't you just wonder what Geoffrey Wiswell's done with his head?" she asked conversationally after Maude brought the peppers and eggs, and Charles had put his work aside. "Giving so much space in *The Spectator* to that Alders Survey drivel?"

"Alders Survey?" Charles repeated, in the detached voice he used when his mind was on something else.

"You ought to have a talk with Geoffrey, Charles. He respects you and listens to you. You ought to speak with him and tell him a family newspaper is no place to print filth, to advertise it."

"Filth? What are you talking about? Since when is Wiswell advertising filth?"

"There's that entire column on page 3 about the Alders people coming to Waymouth next week."

"Alders ... Do you know something? I admit to being double dense when I've had an especially hard week. I just haven't been following it all very much, dear. Let's see. These people are arriving here for two weeks, aren't they? One of their members just died; the head man, if I remember. I'm afraid I haven't kept up with much of it."

Julia told him about it.

"Oh. That's interesting. Well, I hope you have your appointment in early to tell them all they need to know."

"Charles!"

"You go right in there, dear, and burn their ears off. You tell them what an immoral, slatternly wanton you are."

"Now aren't you the comedian!"

He chuckled affectionately and stabbed a curled black pepper with his fork. "You just ask about Charlie Havilland at the Elks. 'Barrel of Laughs Havilland,' Burt Harkness calls me."

"Well, I would *think* you'd find funnier jokes than that. It's far from a funny matter."

"You're right, dear, it is," he agreed amiably, and again she was sure she'd only partially got to him. "I can be free enough to make jokes about it because I can feel free about you. It would take wild horses to make you harm our name and the business by making a spectacle of yourself. This is good as usual, but you might ask Maude next time to go just a drop easier on the salt."

After lunch he drove back downtown. Julia phoned Helen Corbett to suggest an afternoon of bridge or Scrabble, but the maid there told her Mr. and Mrs. Corbett were in Cape May for the weekend. She tried three other friends but they weren't in or had made other plans.

The hardly acceptable fact, that she was being purposely rebuffed by friends who knew her well, irritated her even as she examined it and found that no one was turning away from her wilfully, deliberately. But it was a lovely summer day, a glorious day, and it came to her gradually but with ultimate force that she shouldn't have to spend it alone. She thumbed through her personal address book at her bedroom desk and decided to make calls from the first page and go on down the alphabet. The book was filled with names and numbers, but they belonged to laundries, the Fire and Police Departments, Charles' business associates and their invisible wives, acquaintances whom she barely knew or who had long ago moved from Waymouth. Except for Helen Corbett, and Elizabeth Petrie and less than a handful of others she only occasionally lunched with, she recognized that outside of Charles she hadn't a friend in the world.

Nevertheless, she sat with increasing rigidity at her desk and proceeded to go down the line of the book's alphabet.

By the time she reached the M's she was convinced she was foolish for having let anyone know how indiscreetly she could expose her loneliness, because her voice had commenced to take on that too-high, too-jovially offhand quality. They would replace their receivers and go to their husbands or Saturday bridge games and be cruel. "You should've heard Julia Havilland, the poor thing. She's begging to lick somebody's hand, anybody's. You'd think she'd get after her husband to pay her some mind, or get after someone else to do it. What's she waiting for?"

The tail of Julia's eye caught sight of Marianne Sherwood's name in the book before she closed it. She had thought about her often but had never been able to bring herself around to phone her. She dialed the number now, impetuously and without the vaguest idea of what she would say if the terribly contained Mrs. Sherwood were to answer and ask what she wanted. Mrs. Sherwood, fortunately, wasn't at home. The voice at the other end of the line wasn't sure, but imagined there wouldn't be anyone back before evening, and was there any message? "No, thank you," Julia said. "I'll call again." She hung up and placed the address book in the desk's bottom drawer.

Marianne Sherwood would, without a doubt, be one of the first to volunteer for that horrid survey, thought Julia. But, then, she could do it and get away with it, even if she was Lawrence Sherwood's daughter-in-law. She's radiant and beautiful and she has a way of saying and doing anything outrageous and having everyone admire her for it. I had a nerve, telephoning her. What would I have to say to her if she agreed to see me? That they call my husband 'Barrel of Laughs' Havilland, and isn't that dear?

The rules of proper conduct change slightly, Julia thought as she went back to the lawn and sat with her copy of *Vogue*, when you're someone as animatedly alive as Marianne Sherwood. How wonderful, how incredibly wonderful it would be to be her friend! To hear her tell those saucy stories, to be on hand as a close friend when she needed a friend, to be there for her confidences. It would be better than anything else that's happened to me since—well, since when?

Once more, the thought of Marianne Sherwood carried its belated but resounding association to Mona, and the recollection was a whip at her cheeks. Mona had happened a long, long time ago, at college. It had been dirty then, and the passage of time,

MORTON COOPER

even with the purification of manufactured cleansing fantasy, couldn't make it less dirty.

As always, Julia was able to dismiss the evil thought of Mona when she chose by simply turning to something else. She busied herself in *Vogue* and the benign sun. There no longer was a Mona or a sex survey. There no longer was loneliness, or the happiness she too often lately had idled herself into imagining she had missed, or the outside World of impending and insidious iniquity. There was only peace.

But from nowhere, as one chaste pinafore merged with another on the magazine's pages, the unwelcome fantasy slapped at her and shook her ruthlessly. The dream of fewer than two hours ago returned.

The man's name in the dream hadn't been Erik.

It had been Marianne Sherwood.

Julia stiffened in fright.

CHAPTER THREE

THE FIRST day in Waymouth was the kind of day on which Dr. Alders would have thrived, but Mike Crayne was anxious for it to be over. He disliked what he called setting-up exercises, the administrative tent-pitching which involved meeting the city fathers and persuading them of the worth of the survey over tepid chicken lunches, even though they had been formally invited to come weeks ago. The complaint was not especially valid, Mike realized. The persuasions amounted to little more than shaking civic hands, making a speech when necessary to reinforce the survey's purpose when there appeared to be signs of minor foot-dragging in the community, and wasting a certain amount of time. As Phil said, it was a small enough price to pay; this survey, even with Phil Morrow's shaky theories incorporated, just might go a long way toward completing next winter's report.

The hotel to which they were assigned was no better and no worse than the hotels in other parts of the country; Mike and Phil shared a suite, Nelson had the next single room and Nancy had the single room across the hall. They all set to work immediately, studying the lists of interviewees to which each had been assigned. The response was good and, in terms of group types, not discordantly different from the group types of other cities and towns they visited. Fewer men volunteered than did women and, Herb Graham admitted, were much more secretive about it.

All of them had been screened by Herb and his small staff, and the Jollies—the fringe who gave evidence of volunteering for sick or idle rather than sober purposes—were weeded out and prudently rejected. Phil had asked for ten per cent of teen-agers and they, with their parents' consents, had been supplied by Herb. In Waymouth more than in other places, surprisingly, there were women who agreed to take part in the survey, but only if they could be interviewed by Nancy Garrity; they understood that the men worked with full objectivity, but they were not about to bare themselves to men. Phil didn't approve of the trend, if it was a trend, but confided to Mike that in time they might have to think seriously about increasing the team with more women for the unswayables.

The interview periods were not yet altogether filled, but that never was unusual. Once the snowball descended and the balkers heard that the extraction didn't hurt, there would be far more volunteers than could possibly be honored within a two-week visit.

On the plane to Waymouth, Phil had been absorbed in the Sally Warner story, and had mentioned that it would be a hell of a break if they could get to her for an interview, soon, while the tragedy was still fresh. "We'll get to her doctor right away," he'd said. "If he doesn't anticipate any trouble from an interview this soon afterwards, and if she's agreeable to it, and if her family doesn't raise a squawk, we're in business."

"Those are a lot of if's," Mike had answered. This afternoon, while Phil made his rounds, Mike hunched in his shorts in the suite's bedroom, cradled a Bloody Mary, and tried to reach his wife by long distance. Her line kept busy. Between tries he took a larger and then even larger sip from his drink and, as his disgust built at needing to drink before phoning Valerie, he drank more.

Except for two unrelievedly roof-raising months in college when he'd been drunk almost continually, Mike had never viewed liquor as anything approaching a problem. He had little patience for those who couldn't or wouldn't hold their booze. But here I am, he thought as he poured an inch more vodka into the glass of tomato juice, associating the booze with Valerie. I can't seem to even think of calling her any more without a spot of the jug at my elbow. I have most of my marbles, and if someone were to tell me during an interview that he preferred to telephone his estranged wife only when there was liquor on hand, I'd gather right away that he was in need of some help. Yet here I go, very conscientiously pretending I'm a hopeless stumblebum.

Estranged? That's no word to describe Valerie and me. Nothing radically has changed between us. We love each oth—

Oh, nuts. Stop the kidding. It takes more than half a country to separate two people who love each other. That last long-distance fight of ours was such a howler that it's a wonder the Telephone Company didn't bring charges against us for burning their wires. She told me she was finished with me, that she hated me and the kindest thing I could do for her would be to stay out of San Mateo forever.

Then there had come the air-mail special-delivery letter from her the next day, the letter with the frenetic explanations and the overdone apologies. He had written her that same day rather than called, a long letter of quiet love, assuring her that he was doing his best to understand her emotional flipflops, her abrupt switches from love to hate to love again, and that if she could see her way clear to leave her family long enough to come to him, where she belonged, most of the foolishness would stop instantly.

Their letters crossed. He received another from her the next day, canceling her previous apologies, advising him that she had thought everything through and that they were the original water and oil team. Why was he so pigheaded? When was he going to wake up to see that a divorce was the only thing left to them?

Now, recalling the despicable letter, the clear picture of Valerie returned—the picture of the lovely but spoiled, childish—truculent girl who had begun more and more to believe that growing up was a rude infringement on her rights as a twenty-seven-year-old adolescent—and he decided to hell with attempting to make the call again.

How can I blame her for this kookie conduct when I do so much to encourage it? She gives me the sturdy kick in the groin, waits patiently for me to get back to my knees, and then kicks again.

He heard a knock at the door and thought at once of Phil as he glanced guiltily at the bottle of Smirnoff. Morrow wasn't his boss in the Ebenezer Scrooge sense of the term, and neither were in the habit of answering to one another, but there was the unspoken agreement that drinking—solitary drinking, at least—wasn't part of the schedule. Mike knew he wouldn't have hidden the bottle if Phil were to walk in, anyway, but he was just as glad to remember that Phil never knocked, that he always used his key.

"Come in."

Nancy Garrity entered and waved her small hand, signifying he wasn't to bother to get up, before he had a chance to excuse himself to find a pair of pants.

"I've been trying to get you on the phone," she said after she closed the door, "but your line's been busy and busy."

"Oh? Sit down and peel a few grapes with me," he offered, still not up, smiling and indicating the bottle on the bureau.

"Now, that's what I call a first-rate idea. Here, I'll fix it myself."

"Do that," Mike nodded and slouched into the armchair, raising his legs to the window sill. "We're running a little low on the tomato juice but that can be rectified." He watched the movement of her phenomenally pretty behind as she walked to the bottle and found an empty tumbler. The thought crossed his mind of Nancy as a pleasurable bed partner. He was positive that the very same thought had crossed Phil's mind, too, and, marvel of marvels, maybe even Nelson's, as well. But he was reasonably sure that none of them would ever do anything active about it, and not only because all of them worked so closely together, in physical and professional tight quarters. She owned the kind of marvelously lithe shape his schooldays' dreams had got fat on, and if you were a trace less sensitive to tone and manner you would sometimes get the idea she was inviting such action. But he had seen her and talked with her for roughly five months now and he would have given under oath to a grand jury an opinion that she was a nerve-wracked cake of ice beneath the torrid exterior.

"What's the occasion?" Nancy asked.

"What's what occasion?"

"Peeling the grape all alone at—" she read her watch "ten minutes of four in the afternoon?"

"You sound like Unca Phil would sound if he wanted to make the sound," Mike said, and immediately was sorry he'd said it.

"Do I? I didn't mean to." She built her drink, a cautiously light one, and sat at the edge of the twin bed nearer him. "But it's an occasion, anyway. If I weren't so deathly afraid of being hanged, I'd pack a flask, too, and take a cordial nip before dinner."

"Don't start. I know you, lady doctor. One nip leads to two, and two to eight, and eight leads to carnally attacking the bellboy who delivers the ice cubes, and that leads to all sorts of horrifying things. Like forgetting to send birthday cards."

"You talked me out of it. We couldn't let me take *that* road to vice, could we?" She lifted her glass. "Skol."

"Yeah. Why were you trying to get me on the phone?"

"Oh," she said, and Mike thought he detected a blush rising in her cheeks. "I heard about an extra-special Polynesian restaurant somewhere here in town—you know, with the bacon wrapped around the apples. I thought you might want to try it. Dutch, of course."

"Dutch? You just said Polynesian."

"There's no hurry about it. We'll be here for two weeks."

"Umm, it sounds like a nice idea," Mike asserted and brought himself lazily up from the deep chair as he envisioned Phil waltzing into the bedroom unexpectedly. The nonoccasion cocktail hour was nonconformist enough; the view of him sharing it in his shorts with a female colleague would take a bit of explaining. As well it should, he told himself as he sauntered toward his pants, a few feet away from Nancy. He would doubtless raise a spinsterish eyebrow himself if he were to catch Morrow in the same situation. You kept up decent appearances, even on safari. "What happened to Nelson? I thought you and he unwrapped bacon at mealtime."

"Nelson?"

"Don't you two have your dinners together?"

"Now you're sounding like Louella Parsons with an exclusive, and a false one, at that. Nelson and I pair off together, Dr. Crayne, as often as we do only because you and Phil are forever eating soggy corned-beef sandwiches in rooms like this, and at the strangest hours. What do you propose we do, climb back into the trees after hours?"

Buckling his belt at the far side of the room, Mike laughed aloud, momentarily puzzled by the frank way she observed what he was doing. He elected not to pursue it.

"Where's Nelson now?" he inquired. "Giving them a hard time at the public library?"

"Don't be nasty."

"Nasty? Then educate me. Doesn't he head for the public library every time we get to a new place? To study the terrain in all the local archives? Is that being nasty?"

"As a matter of fact, that's exactly where he is. But you have an old biddy way about you—you know that, don't you? —that makes 'Hello, how are the folks?' nasty when you say it."

"I'll cut out my serpent tongue," Mike said as he returned to her and the Smirnoff, "but first I'll apply a drop more of this antifreeze." Her drowsy, floating perfume was a touch more pungent than he'd ever remembered it being during working hours, and he couldn't quite shake off the tight-throated feeling that she hadn't dropped in here merely to ask him to share dinner with her.

He freshened her glass, over her admirably feeble protests, and Valerie's fruity, long-distance perfume filled his inner nostrils. Quit the homy stuff, Romeo, he cautioned. It's your missus you're missing. The missus you're going to get back. A while away from her and you start climbing walls, you fantasy that Sophia Loren's warm for your slouchy form.

"We haven't had much of a chance to talk, Nancy," Mike said, sitting again. She had hardly moved. "Since you joined this band of gypsies, we've been leaping from one carnival to the next, except for the Doctor's bonfire." He wanted to take the last part of the sentence back, too, when he noticed how it had made her start. She had had a deep respect for Victor Alders. Mike Crayne's respect had been longer, and perhaps greater if only because of its length, but generations of Craynes made a diligent point of masking those feelings that were strongest. He paused, as if to let her know he was paying his fleeting penance, and then went on. "Do you think we make sense? Going from one cultural spa to another, chasing down renegade libidos and writing X's beside them, I mean?"

"Certainly I do. Don't you?"

"Ah-ah. I'm the interviewer, Miss."

"And the vice-president in charge of queries."

"Stool pigeon, you mean? Don't give me that hogwash. I'm a clock-puncher, same as you. Nothing you say will be held against you." He had an urge to add the dirty joke, but chose to postpone it for a more propitious time. What the hell, he thought, maybe I've gone too far already and she hasn't been here five minutes.

Nancy gave him a sweet, absolutely mockingless smile. "I can still give you honest testimony. I believe in what Dr. Alders set out to do. I believe in what we're doing. I hate to sound as though

I'm Florence Nightingale, but I wouldn't stay with the Institute for a day if I didn't believe that what I was doing was useful."

"Enough said. You passed the final exam. You may now take sophomore physics." The next vaguely demonic urge was to sound her out on her attitude about Morrow's new plans, but he let it go. It was bad pool. It didn't belong, obviously not at this point. "How's your drink doing?"

"I can hardly lift it. How were you able to pour an entire quart from a fifth?"

He laughed again, liking her. "That's the mad scientist's secret," he maintained. "I know sophomore trigonemetry. All you know is sophomore physics. Don't dare to ask the mad scientist stupid questions."

They had started to ask each other where Phil was, when Phil turned the knob, finding the door unlocked, and came in. For an instant Mike felt like the naughty kid caught experimenting with corn silk, and hated himself for the feeling. What ceilings would cave in? He had fixed himself an afternoon slug and had invited Nancy Garrity to join him. Obviously Phil Morrow wasn't about to spank him. He was quickly sorry for Nancy, though. Sitting on a man's bed with her gorgeous legs crossed, with a large drink in her small hand, the blush in her face he had imagined earlier was now an extention in color of the tomato juice. Phil's surprise at seeing her here was natural and swiftly gone, but there was no doubt that she was visibly embarrassed. He wished he could say something that wouldn't turn him into an everlasting jerk.

"What's the celebration?" Phil asked, without guile, undoing his tie and removing his seersucker jacket. The day had become abnormally hot and the suite's air conditioner had temporarily conked out. One day they will ask us folks from the Alders Institute to describe the greatest hardships of our lives, Mike thought, and we will tell them: The moment the weather turned hot, the air conditioners in the best hotels conked out.

"Nancy dropped in a few minutes ago to ask the same question, more or less," Mike replied. "I told her I was drinking a summer toast to General Hamilton Sherwood's memory. The Sherwoods were the first recorded family in Waymouth. It says so on the desk blotter."

"If there's anything left in the jug, I'll be only too happy to toast his memory, too," Phil advised and threw his jacket on one of the straight chairs. "Wow, but this has been a big day so far. And it's not over yet. You'll be delighted to know we're all expected to meet The Waymouthites at seven tonight for dinner at Waymouth Hall. Several educators and ministers will address us and we will address them. Somebody will play "In the Hall of the Mountain King," and a fat lady with green beads will render "Mighty Lak a Rose." Don't nobody make a rush for the exit or I shoot."

"I'm taking the words right out of Nancy's mouth," Mike grumbled and handed Phil the remainder of the bottle. "Damn it to hell."

"Those aren't my words," Nancy complained with no sign of complaint in her eyes. "My words are unrepeatable in front of gentlemen."

"Can't help it," Phil shrugged. "To get maximum cooperation, we have to start out fraternizing with the original enemy. Don't worry, kids. I've cased this joint called Way-mouth, New York. The recalcitrants are around, for sure, but Dr. Alders wouldn't even have bothered to roll up his sleeves. Herb Graham did a terrific job of selling us, and there're plenty of good people in this old town. The road-blocks won't be major, the way they used to be. We'll be swimming, from here on in."

"If I'm expected to go through one more of those civic functions with the fat ladies with the green beads, coach," Mike said leisurely, scratching his ankle, "I'm putting in for overtime."

"Which reminds me," Phil added, sitting beside Nancy who, Mike observed, had only just now begun to unblush, "where's

Nelson? I thought I saw him in the lobby and I called, but I was wrong."

"He should be back soon," Nancy put in. "He's at the library."

Softly spoken, it was a family joke, cruel but affectionate, and apparently Phil had no desire to play it up. He talked, instead, of what had happened since he'd left them after breakfast, when they'd been given the Waymouth studies to go over, preparatory to tomorrow morning's first sessions in Waymouth Hall. He had met with everyone of local consequence, and had been assured of all-out success. He had done better than he would have thought with the Warner girl, the girl who had been raped.

"You have one of your biggest jobs cut out for you, Nancy," he declared. "You've been blessed with interviewing Sally Warner."

"I?"

"Let's not fight over prize bones. I would've given my one good tooth to have had her on my list, but she says *if* she's going to talk at all, it will be with her own gender. I have the sneaking hunch that means you."

"My courtly thanks," Nancy nodded, and Mike noted she wasn't particularly pleased.

"I might as well fill you in now with the rudiments, because this is big, possibly bigger than anything the others have attempted."

"Phil, if you're thinking of my doing counseling," Nancy pleaded, "please count me out. I'm a big, smart girl, but I wouldn't try to—"

"I didn't ask for that. You'll ask the questions and take the data, the same as if she were Brand X. I'll be hovering in the wings. I'll be around for the rough times."

"All right."

"It was no picnic," said Phil. "She's home from the hospital, and her doctor—he's an awfully fine guy, named Maslyn—had no objection to her coming onto the court if she gave her okay. But I had to battle with her father, who's a dyed-in-the-wool maniac, and with her older sister Frances, who's not appreciably far behind. When I finally got to see her, she didn't seem at first to be much better than the others. No soap. We wanted to pry, we wanted to learn her filthy secret and broadcast it to the world. Well, I repeated Dr. Maslyn's name, and it cut some of the cards—"

"And so did your ineffable charm," Mike interrupted, quoting the women's magazines with feigned mockery.

"My charm was monumental. Anyway, Nancy, if she does show up at noon on Tuesday as she three-quarters-of-the-way promises, are you game?"

"What's the game?" Nancy chuckled, finally rising from her stiltedly perched position on the bed's edge and placing the half-filled glass on the nearest surface. "Russian Roulette?"

"That could be," said Phil without humor.

"Yes," Nancy agreed. "I'll be there."

Thinking no one saw him, Phil rubbed his hands. Then he rose, forgetting his drink, and grinned. "We're in business," he approved.

"I'm going back to my room for a shower and a short nap," she announced. "I'll be ready when you're ready. Just ring twice,"

"Good, Nancy. Good."

Once she had gone, Mike Crayne helped himself to a fresh view of the party poop who had cracked into his idyll. You are growing old for thirty-three, my friend, he thought. You are taking on Dr. Alders' least happy mannerisms in too quick a time, and you are becoming Mr. Hyde before you've altogether learned how to be Dr. Jekyll.

And why don't I have guts enough to tell you to be yourself, to cut out the crap before it buries you?

You're playing Big Daddy, and you don't yet look right for the part.

"She looks mighty tasty, that girl," said Phil, a trifle self-consciously, more self-conscious than he had sounded a month ago when he had bitched, along with the others, about Dr. Alders' funny ways.

"Those were my thoughts, too, in a general way," Mike said evenly. "Tell me, sport: do you think she puts out?"

"I wouldn't doubt it," Phil Morrow said in an absent voice. "Mike, let me tell you about this town. Let me tell you about this Warner girl ... "

In her hotel room, Nancy Garrity stripped until she was naked.

Advancing across the spare room, unleashing the tiny hair ribbon so that her massive hair fell to her shoulders, she passed the bureau mirror and saw her reflection with alarm. Her face looked no different from the way it had in their bedroom, and her body did not tremble as she was sure it had trembled then, but she had never been so conscious of falling apart. Of quite literally opening at all the wrong seams and waiting for the sawdust to pour recklessly to the floor.

She flung herself on the lonely bed which accentuated the anonymity of the room and prepared to cry, but there was no suitable reason to do it. The ball was marble in her throat and a chill made her bare shoulders shudder, but crying was useless.

There had been those kinds of girls in Minneapolis. The grandstand players. She had witnessed them at high school soirees and at the outside parties and all through her years at college. The nice girls from the refined families, not the open tramps. You would stand out of sight and look at them, see the sexual aggressiveness in their otherwise restrained glances, see the way they invited boys to undress them without uttering a word or even smiling evilly. They were worse than the open tramps because they honestly believed they were gifts from the refined gods, that they could have it both ways by being whores with their eyes and ladies with their names.

Nancy thought of the two men across the hall and dug her face into the pillow. They're sitting there this minute, she told herself, talking about me and laughing at me. If I'd had any quality to me, I would never have gone into his room until I was sure he was fully dressed. I didn't only sit with him, I gave him that ridiculous stare as he got up and started to dress. I was inviting him to take me, right there, right then.

And he knew it, he sensed it!

As soon as Phil Morrow assigned me to the Sally Warner case, I should have instantly taken myself off it. "No particular reason, Phil, I just won't take it on." The similarity between us is too great. I'll never stand up under it. The active Tweedledee will naively seek help from the passive Tweedledum. It's impossible, and the results will show up fast. Rape, nothing. We are the nice girls, the retiring girls who slap freshman cheeks in the rear seats of cars after dances. We are not the open tramps. We cry rape because it's such a tidy, all-inclusive, unimplicating word, and in crying it we remove the onus we'd played eyesies for in the first vulgar place.

There is true rape in the backwash countries and among the faceless folks in countries nobody's ever heard of, but it's a fraudulent word in civilization, she assured herself as she forced herself up to rest on an elbow. It is fantasy or the extension of fantasy, and when the chips are down among us higher animals, what's the difference?

Curtsying respectfully to the realistic fact of unreality, she still had always hated her mother for dying so early, for moving her bedroom so close to Daddy's bedroom in a house too big to hold only a flawless father and a young, needful daughter. ("Daddy, when I grow up, do you know what I'm going to do? I'm going to marry you." "That's nice, punkin. We'll see, we'll see.") Daddy kept busy at his work, his silly work. He would have his business people in during the evenings. He would pick her up, swing her around, kiss her in front of all his business people, and call out, "This beautiful young lady has only one ambition. She has the idea she's going to marry me one day." They would all laugh.

The library was nicest at that hour, half-past seven, when she had to leave it. It was the nicest room in the big house. It wasn't too large like the other rooms, and it was warm and cozy with firelight and the sounds of voices. The paneling seemed to absorb the soft light and the voices and to be mellow with them. The bronze leopard on the mantle knew her and was friendly, and the books with their red and blue and green covers were her friends. She liked the wide, comfortable sofa and its soft cushions that smelled faintly of tobacco and mothballs when you buried your nose in them, the overstuffed chair where her father sat, and her mother's rocker.

The fantasies grew to wild dimensions when her Uncle Jason stopped by every fall for two weeks. By the time she had reached fourteen (*the horrid chuck under the chin, the lingering stare at the growth of her young breasts, the awkward, throat-clearing talk about how fullsomely she'd grown*) she had entirely transferred her love for her father to her Uncle Jason. In the loneliness of her darkened room, away from the saved teddy bear and the autographed photograph of Alan Ladd up there on her bureau, the images flowed. He stole into the room, pressed his manicured nail to her sensuous lips, and begged her to be quiet as a mouse. He threaded toward her, brought her up into his powerful arms, kissed her mouth, and pleaded with her to keep this their own, private secret.

"It isn't right," she breathed.

"But how can it be wrong?" he muttered.

She accepted him in her dream, and enjoyed his enjoyment of her. They had all laughed at her and she had timidly giggled back, but now there was no need to giggle any longer. At precisely the right moment, she rose from the bed, thrust his aged hands away, and cried out: "Rape! Help! Rape!"

The fantasy, for a reason she never had allowed herself to follow, had clogged at just that point. She would think of her father angrily bursting into the dark room and switching on thousands of lights, but she would refuse to make herself see it....

Her telephone rang.

"This is Nelson, Nancy."

"Oh, yes, Nelson," she said, and watched her free hand foolishly bring the pillow up from the bed to cover her breasts.

"I'm just about leaving the library now. If you think you know it all about American history, you ought to dip into a few of these musty old books here. Everything happened here."

"I'll bet."

"Say, I heard about this fabulous restaurant in town, out on a place called Underwood Road. It's genuine Polynesian, and it's called Loy-Loy Luau. The prices aren't too steep. What do you say to our trying it before the Waymouthite dinner? You know what sort of meal we'll get there—lumpy, cold potatoes."

"The Waymouthite dinner?"

"I called the hierarchy room. They said you were there and you knew all about it."

"Oh. Yes."

"So what's the good word?"

"I—thought we might—all go there."

"All?" Nelson disparaged. "Mutt and Jeff, too? Excuse the expression, if they're listening in. Phil has Mike closed up in conference till zero hour, meaning the Waymouthite dinner. That will be some day when we all get together for dinner."

"All right, then, Nelson. Ah—it's getting late, and we'd do best to hurry it up. I can shower and be in the lobby in twenty minutes."

"Righto," Nelson said and hung up.

The icy shower helped to revive her, to wipe out most of the bad thoughts, and when she reached for the hotel Turkish towel she felt as if she could cope with most crises, as long as she wasn't expected to look at her mirror image. The radio was playing a surprisingly soft "Malagueña," and that helped, too.

Her father, Ian Garrity, once had written, "Scientifically the word 'oversexed' does not exist, nor does the word 'undersexed'. One gives and gets or one does not give and get; it is as unquestionably easy as that."

This remembrance helped most of all. You still know everything, she thought.

You could set your watch, the neighbors on Griswold Street liked to say, by Will Warner's comings and goings. Except for two nights a week and for two weeks in July, he opened the front door of his brown frame house at precisely fifteen minutes before ten in the evening, and exactly ten minutes later he checked into the rear entrance of Sherwood's, where he diligently punched the clock and proceeded to make the rounds of all five floors of the department store. At ten minutes past six he checked out again, having done a good night-watchman's job, and within the next quarter hour he would visit, without fail, The Grandsons of Bull Run on South Main Street, the private club which served drinks to any of its members at any hour.

By 8:00 A.M. he would be dourly drunk, oversensitively wound up for an argument, but everyone would jolly him and advise him to go home and sleep it off. Nodding agreeably, he would leave the club by 8:30, tip his hat to elderly ladies with a crusty outer worldliness, and stagger home. He would get there at nine o'clock, on the dot.

The housewives on Griswold Street would peek through their kitchen windows, see him come down the block at a sea-going gait, and know it was time for the nine o'clock news on the radio.

The Sherwood family, as well as the long-time Griswold residents, knew that Will Warner ("Hasn't he aged fast?" "That mangy, cantankerous old buzzard? He was a filthy old man when he was seventeen!") was a drinker, but no one ever had the time or inclination to call him on the carpet for it. Year after year, no one would ever accuse him of being drunk on the job or on the way to the job. What he did after he left work was his own business.

Sally Warner knew that the neighbors and the in-spite-of-themselves people at Sherwood's regarded her father with a little impatience but with a grudging affection. They heard the reason for his drunkenness so often that reality had blossomed into mammoth myth and he had become the object of spontaneous sympathy. He'd not always been a night watchman, a clock puncher. The Warners had lived in Waymouth for generations, long before The Outsiders had taken it over, and one of the most famous of Civil War ancestors was buried up there in Bridgewell Park. Will had been a respectable businessman, with his own stationary and cigar store on Cheshire Avenue, and made a nice living until his wife Nola died delivering Sally. He'd been crazy about Nola, the legend went, and he'd gone half-crazy with her death, poor soul. Her passing had brought on the drinking. You could understand if you'd ever known Nola, claimed the Griswold Street long-timers. An absolute saint. Hair of spun gold, a face and figure right out of a movie magazine, and there never was a more devoted couple.

The knowledge of the myth, hearing it gradually build and build out of proportion, had once disturbed Sally. Little of it, she and her older sister Frances knew, was true. Will Warner's two-by-four cigar counter had just about never been a paying proposition, largely because he was seldom there to attend it. He had always been mean. He had married Nola Durand only because he had not been able to marry an already married woman from Brooklyn. He had been angered rather than made disconsolate by her death, and had worked a great deal of mileage, over the past twenty-one years, from publicly proclaiming his tremendous loss. The facts of his punctuality and earnestness at Sherwood's were true, Sally could concede. But he also was rigid and nasty, drunk or sober, vicious and contemptuous and ill-humored, unnecessarily domineering.

He controlled Frances to the point where Frances was ever ready to jump through a hoop.

He will never do that to me, Sally had decided a least a year ago.

Sitting up in bed, taking borrowed breaths as she waited for Frances to switch off the hall light and close her own bedroom door, Sally wondered if this was how an otherwise normal person went mad; if one breaking point brought on insanity, or if she had been stealthily leading up to it long before the evening with Bob in Bridgewell Park. Until that night, she had been fairly secure in her reputation. A nice enough girl, friendly, a trifle too moody once in a while for the big men on the basketball squad, but a girl shrewd enough not to professionalize her virginity.

Since that night, everything had changed, and there had been no one but Frances and Dr. Maslyn to tell her differently. She had wanted nothing so much as to be held by Daddy, to weep and to have him understand her. She had even tried, as Dr. Maslyn had confidentially suggested. The weeping had embarrassed Daddy and turned him mean again. He had reddened, loudly cursed his luck, called her vile names. This morning, when he had come home from The Grandsons of Bull Run, he had bawled her out. His wrath had been so vehement, so nearly incoherent, that the idea had crossed her mind that someone at the saloon had fed him the words. He had railed on about her being bad and soiled and just like her mother, and then he had slapped her across her face.

Through the long day she had needed to tell someone, any-one, what had happened. She had thought to tell Frances whom she loved and trusted, the sister who was so unfailingly selfless, who had stood by her throughout the week's nightmare, who hadn't once questioned her motive for going to the park that night. But Frances had come home from work at the gas com-pany, and Sally had been unable to form the words. Guv Barnes, the boy who had been in the senior class when Sally was a fresh-man, had phoned at noon and asked, out of a clear blue sky, to see her for a date, and at the time it had seemed like a good idea. She had a dim recollection of what people said about Guv, but a clear recollection of what he looked like. He worked at the Arbrought foundry, and there were the scratchy rumors going around from the years at high school that he was something of a bum, that he had made one of the Polish girls from just outside the City pregnant and then had left her. But he was, Annette Jablonski and Helene Brenner from the store agreed, almost unendurably handsome. Sally had seen him from time to time on Main Street, a Lassiterville boy grown this side of squat but with muscles that didn't apologize for rippling, and her second-story-window crush on him had stalled for an excessively long time. Until she had met Bob.

Finally, Sally saw the hall light go off and heard Frances' door softly close. That meant Daddy had left for work, Frances had entombed herself for the night, and within fifteen minutes the coast would be clear.

She slipped out of bed and brought the good faille over her head, feeling all the while that she indeed was going crazy. She dug her tiny feet into brown moccasins, combed her hair in the semi-dark, and dropped the comb and a lipstick into a pocket.

She opened her door and listened. Frances' light went out and in a minute there was silence. Frances, who seldom had any-thing to say, would brag that she could summon sleep by merely placing her head on a pillow, and hear nothing ever again but her alarm clock.

The waiting was incalculably endless, but gradually it became time and then Sally found herself in the rear of the Griswold Street house. Guv sat in the front seat of his dusty Ford, wearing a T-shirt with the white cotton sleeves rolled up as high as they would go to show off his sledge-hammer muscles.

Except for a few tell-tale lines at his forehead, and those bulgy pouches beneath his eyes, he hadn't changed at all since high school. He was sullenly but startlingly handsome. His crinkly hair still reminded her of Brillo. As she closed the door after her, she remembered the stories about the Polish girl he had made pregnant.

They were hateful, if they were true. But then, she thought, I'm being hateful, too. I know what he is and what he called me for. I could have stayed home, the way Dr. Maslyn told me to do. I didn't. Guv Barnes phoned me, and I know why Guv Barnes phones a girl, and I said yes.

Where's there anyone to advise me, from here on in?

"You took your sweet time, kid," he said, lazily lowering his fingers to the ignition. "What'd you do, stay for the prayer meeting?"

"Can we go now, Guv?" she asked.

"Go," he repeated. There was a wooden grin on his thin, pinched lips. "Yeah. We go."

The Ford pulled out, raced mercilessly over the ribbons of back roads and, as he talked his small talk, Sally could feel the inexplicable impulse to go back home. The idea had been so right when he had telephoned her and given her his creamy voice. All of it was wrong now.

"What's your pleasure kid?" he inquired. "Beer and dogs at Smoky's? The planetarium? Open-air movie outside Lassiter-ville?"

"The movie sounds good, if we're not too late. Do you know what's playing, Guv?"

Guv shrugged his wide shoulders as he drove, and Sally sensed that he had no feeling, one way or another, about her being here. They would settle into one spot at the drive-in. They would watch the movie for a while. The proper time would pass, and then he would reach for her.

She would resist him. There would be ugly words and—

No. There wouldn't be any ugly words at all. She had known Guv Barnes from her freshman year. She had known what kind of boy he was, and there was nothing to show he had changed since then.

There was no clear blue sky. He had called her today, instead of all the other days and all the other years, for a particular purpose. Sally Warner was fair game. Guv Barnes knew it. Daddy knew it. Frances, her sister, would die before saying so, but Frances imagined it. And if I agreed to see him out of that blue sky, she thought, I knew it most of all.

"You—uh—had a rugged time over there in the park last week, didn't you," Guv said, not asked.

"Well…"

"They caught the wop, though. That's somep'm."

"Guv…"

"Yeah."

"I think I made a mistake. I saw that movie at the drive-in. Let's turn back, okay?"

"You saw it? Which movie? What's its name?"

"I don't remember the name, but I saw it. Can we go back?"

They rode to The Lido, and Guv paid the fare. He inched up the lane to the farthest free space, and Sally saw Laurence Harvey and Geraldine Page in a vigorous wide-screen embrace. Guv, grinning straight ahead, relaxed by flexing his muscled arm over the top of the seat, and dropping his hand on Sally's shoulder.

"Guv—"

"You can never tell when the spooks'll come on the screen to scare you. You need me to protect you."

His hand was both meaningless and hurtful. Sally remembered sitting up in bed at a quarter of ten, sipping warm milk and conscientiously ignoring the nembutal tablet Dr. Maslyn had advised her to take. She could hear snatches of Frances' quiet voice and Daddy's raucous voice at the foot of the stairs. She had told Frances nothing about the unexpected slap, but Frances had known there had been words.

"It just wasn't right, Dad, what you said to Sally before. Dr. Maslyn ordered her to rest and told us not to say anything that would upset her. You shouldn't've said what you said."

"What're you, tellin' me how to behave in my own house? This here's a black mark on my name—folks lookin' at me like they're astin' what kind of a daughter'd I bring up—and I got no intention of lettin' her forget it. And you keep outta tryin' to order me around!"

"Shhh! She's sleeping."

"Don't you shush me! If she'd been sleepin' where she belonged that night, I could still walk through the streets like a gentleman and hold my head up! You're not to shush me ever again!"

"Guv," Sally said now, "can I tell you what happened? Can I tell you all about it?"

"Sure, kid."

"Without you touching me like that?"

"Who's touching you? Talk. Go."

It was all so terribly wrong, every bit of it. It was no better than trying to reach Daddy. Only Daddy, for all his wallops, wasn't after what Guv Barnes was after.

"I knew this boy. Bob Raymond."

"Sure, kid."

"He taught mechanical drawing at High. His mother hates me. She thinks I had something to do with—"

"You know mothers. The big play."

"Guv. Please listen. Please."

"So I'm listening," he nodded, as his hand snaked over her shoulder and somehow got to the hook of her bra.

"Guv—"

"We unfasten there, and let's see what happens here."

The obscenity was that his eyes never left the screen ahead. She could feel the brassiere slither down her blouse and hit the half-slip. She could feel the buttons unbuttoning at her back, one by one, and his large, frigid hand sliding over it and trickling to the front as he viewed Geraldine Page speaking her piece up on the leviathan screen.

There was still time to free herself, she suspected, and no more harm would be done than she had brought on herself till now. There was no surprise at what he was doing, but there was a keen disappointment that he had begun so quickly, a sweeping fear that she had for him no face, no name. She had known this was going to happen, had wanted it to happen. But not this way. Not this fast, not so ruthlessly without love.

"Guv, you—mustn't rush me," she said shyly.

He chuckled, but he wouldn't stop.

"Come here, kid. We're out of high school a long, long time now. That 'don't rush me' flap went out with nursery rhymes, and you know it."

"I don't know—"

His free arm encircled her and he muttered, "Now you start growin' up for real," just before his mouth searched hers. He was rough, unaware of her, and for a moment she was uncontrollably lost in giddiness and in the brutality of his desire.

His head pulled back slightly and in the darkness she could make out the smile of an approving lover.

"You"'re a knockout, kid. You sure know your way around town.

"Don't talk, please don't talk. Kiss me."

"Like the end," he chuckled, teasing her. "A second ago you were getting salty because you wanted us to talk."

"Please…"

"Let's get the show on the road. You must be sensational, for the boy friend to walk the plank for you in Bridgewell last week."

Her spirit shuddered. She met his mouth unflinchingly with her red lips that were warm and beautiful and most scornfully dead.

She brought his hand out from inside her dress, forced herself away, and sat erect. "Thank you for everything, Guv. Now take me home."

His eyes narrowed but he made no move for her. "You better say that again. I only speak English."

"I said I want you to take me home."

"Barnes got hisself a kook tonight, didn't he?"

"Are you going to start the car?"

"What the hell's bugging you?"

"Are we leaving?"

There was an ominous pause, and she was grateful that he had begun to retreat to his place at the wheel.

"You get your bucket out of my car, lady," he told her evenly. "On the double."

Sally looked at him.

"I'm gonna say it once more before I cut your heart out. The name happens to be Barnes, not Milquetoast. You slice outta here pronto or I'm gonna make what happened last week look like a church picnic."

The lonely walk on the path to the drive-in's entrance shamed her, and she was certain that those in their cars who weren't watching the movie or weren't consumed in their own private research were eyeing her. She thought to call for a taxi at the box office, but the box office had closed for the night and she could detect no one who looked as if he belonged to the theatre. She made her way down the drive-in's ramp, regarded the highway which seemed to stretch out to nothing but pitch, and tried to get her bearings. Waymouth was to the right, at least five miles away.

It was late. The thought struck her that even if she were to find a telephone, the town's one taxi service might be closed.

Recalling an Esso station about a half-mile away, Sally began to walk toward it, keeping to the side of the highway, hopefully out of sight of passing cars. An open-top roadster slowed down. She saw two young men in the front seat and her heart lurched. Their invitation to drive her to where she was heading seemed reasonable enough, but she refused them. The regret set in as soon as they sped into the night.

Before long, she thought, I will meet the lady from the Alders Survey. If I am ever to work myself out of this nightmare, I will tell her right out what I did tonight. She will ask what it was like to see Bob murdered, what it was like to be taken, in violence, by a man I had never seen before, and I will tell her truthfully that nothing more hideous could happen to anyone.

She will ask if I knew Guv Barnes' reputation. I will say yes. She will ask why I agreed to meet him, after dark, in the dark, in secret.

There is no answer to that.

Daddy called me a slut. How can I tell her, or anyone, that he's wrong, that he just doesn't understand? Yet slut is a girl who finds herself on a dusty, starless road at midnight, miles from her home and bed, so nearly petrified with fright that soon there will be no feeling left at all.

And what will the lady from the survey say when she hears there soon will be no feeling?

By the time she exhaustedly reached the lighted service station, three cars had slowed down or stopped to offer her a lift. The fear that she would meet someone she knew, someone who would question her being alone this late at night out in nowhere's middle, made her keep her face in shadow. There were two cars waiting for gas as she padded to the pay telephone at the side of the station. She was positive she looked like a dragged cat, and prayed she wouldn't be recognized.

She had just begun to fumble in her purse for a dime when she heard, "Miss Warner!"

She turned and saw Mr. Sherwood, in his yellow Thunderbird, only a few feet away.

I couldn't have planned it more disastrously if I tried, she thought. But then, she added, I did try, didn't I?

He was getting out of the car and coming toward her, a tall and spotless man in his middle thirties. In the store he passed her counter every day but only rarely talked to her. If her picture hadn't been in *The Spectator*, she believed, he likely wouldn't have recognized her away from her counter.

"Well, my eyes didn't deceive me, after all," he said, and Sally watched him carefully for a sign of unfriendliness. "It's you."

"Yes," Sally said weakly. "I was about to call for a cab."

"Is there any trouble?"

"Ah—no. No trouble."

"Where do you live?"

"On Griswold Street. Near Arbrought's."

Mr. Sherwood nodded. "You'll probably wait here all night for a taxi. And this isn't the place to wait alone. Come on. I'll drop you."

"Oh, thanks, Mr. Sherwood, but I can—"

"Come on. No problem."

Riding toward town, she had to think fast, and decided to tell him simply that she had gone on a date, that the boy had got a little out of hand and that she had chosen to walk home. The explanation appeared to satisfy him, for he didn't pursue it. He was interested in her, kindly and solicitous without once getting overbearing, and for moments at a time she forgot that she worked for him. At the store, he always seemed removed, a trifle pompous. But here, now, without the Sherwood legend to back him up, he was altogether human and likable. Just before they reached Arbrought's, he remembered that he had spent the evening at the Country Club but hadn't had a bite to eat since five o'clock. Would she have a sandwich and a cup of coffee with him?

They found a quiet all-night diner and took a booth in the rear. They spent an hour together and, she realized with surprise later, the time flew. Their conversation touched often on Bridgewell Park, but gently; he never pressed, never leered, and he was so supportive that Guv Barnes had never existed.

At her home, he asked to see her again. She heard herself agree. As she undressed for bed, she recalled not only that he was her boss, but that he was married. She had seen Mrs. Sherwood a number of times. Mrs. Sherwood was a beautiful woman, a movie actress who had been in a picture with Susan Hayward, and everyone in town knew that the Sherwoods were happily married.

Sinking into a restless sleep, Sally Warner tried to visualize what the lady from the Alders Survey looked like.

❧ ❧ ❧

Marianne didn't know what to make of Julia Havilland's phone call at eleven in the morning. It was a rambling, disconnected call, replete with chairlady of the board refinement, but somehow muddled. Between the odd ah's and er's, Marianne got the idea that Julia was lonely, wanted company because Charles Havilland had left town for a convention in some distant country called Spokane, and was there any possibility of their getting together for dinner one of these evenings?

"Why one of these evenings?" Marianne scoffed. "Why not make it today? Come see me for cocktails at five."

Replacing the receiver, she suspected with scorn that she ought next to put on a Mother Hubbard, buy a rocking chair, and go to work in a settlement house. Irons were in the Marianne Sherwood fire, important irons, and it had been crazy to invite The Frump Lady over to swap platitudes. Only the confused confession of loneliness from Julia had encouraged the invitation. Marianne had felt loneliness, felt it so stingingly that it could have been tasted.

For the fourth time since late yesterday afternoon, she placed her two calls: one to Aaron Miles at the Hotel Plaza, and one to Aaron Miles at the New York offices of his Hollywood studio. By now the people at both places recognized her voice, and the secretary at the hotel told her, ever so sweetly and patiently, "I've told you, Miss Terrin. I've given Mr. Miles your messages. He likes to talk with everyone, but he's an extremely busy man and it's—"

"Everyone?" she cut in. "Maybe I didn't make myself clear the last time we talked, Miss. I had a featured role in *Sons of Solomon*. It's not as though—"

"I'll see that he gets this message, too, Miss Terrin. Forgive me now; there're other calls waiting."

The sudden impatience knocked her off balance and soon the vague jitters commenced. The morning blast of vodka didn't help at all. It was inconceivable—well, wasn't it?—that he wouldn't contact her. He had a reputation as the most venemous institution since the S.S. Elite Guard, but her association with him had been pleasant. He had fought with Hayward, but he had taken time to be complimentary to Marianne Terrin. He had even told her at the completion of *Sons of Solomon* that he trusted she would work with him again.

To see all possibilities through, she made calls to the few remaining big fixers she knew in the City, the ones who could cut through the red tape of sassy secretaries and sucker fish and get to Miles. They were either not in, or informed her they couldn't do anything for her. When she saw herself pouring a third vodka before brunch and then starting to pace the floors like a caged movie actress, the jitters truly visited. At the risk of tying up the line and missing Miles' call, she phoned Dan Parrish, who lately was always miraculously available to her. She let the telephone ring eight times, but there was no reply.

The liquor was taking its lazy old time in snapping to and becoming her pal today, but by half-past four it edged up to offer its peaceable effect. She had not bothered to change from her pink silk pajamas, nor had she bothered to down anything sturdier than a slice of toast and a cup of Mrs. Quigley's abominable black coffee. Eunice must have sensed this was Warpath Day, because she announced lunch twice and then discreetly took to the hills of the kitchen.

The nice vodka had begun to film her senses and contentedly slow her reflexes when Mrs. Quigley poked her dishonorable head in and informed her, "Phone for you. Mr. Sherwood."

"Thank you," she acknowledged and stopped before she picked up the receiver to test her coherency under her breath. "Steve's shaggy sport shirt," she recited. It would have won a diction award.

"Hello," she said.

"How are you, dear?"

"Good as new. To what do I owe this call, Steven? Or is it Christmas again so soon?"

"You've chosen your weapons," Steve said drily.

"Not at all. I'm glad to hear your voice. I was sitting here trying to remember what it sounded like."

"Let's have half a minute more of this witty banter, and then I'll tell you why I phoned."

"I'm all out of jokes. Get up on that Mount, Steven, and let's hear the Sermon. You do it so well."

"I was under the impression we had a long talk not so long ago about that bottle you're hitting. You were going to cut it down."

"Who says I'm hitting the bottle?"

"Oh, stop it, Marianne. You never think to get this bitchy when you're sober. I'm calling with a pretty good idea for tonight. If you want to keep giving me these second-act-curtain lines, then I'll go back to work and you can write them all down for me. I'll read them when I get home."

"Who's making the witty banter now?"

"Do you want to hear the idea?"

"It's your phone call."

"Eddie Moran can get me two fourth-row-center seats for the Merman show tonight," Steve stated with what she had to admit was nobly controlled calm. "We haven't been to a show together in ages. I thought we might have some dinner at Twenty-One, and then go for some potato pancakes at Luchow's afterwards." He paused. "How does it sound?"

"I'd better contact a private detective, first thing in the morning."

"Now how in the hell is that supposed to answer my question?" he barked, and she knew there was no answer to his question.

She tried. "Shouldn't a wife contact a private detective when her husband unexpectedly brings her flowers? The last time you invited me out for a night like this was the week after they shot old Honest Abe."

She could see him, across the acres of telephone lines, frowning and digging his fingernails into his desk. There had been no call to say what she'd said, but she had never learned how to apologize.

The silence was deadening, but finally he answered her.

"Go back to your bottle, Marianne," he declared, his voice purposely unruffled. "It's good for you. It'll make you big and strong and keep you company." He caught his breath. "And while you're swimming in it, do us all a favor. Drown."

Click.

Marianne sat deep in the brown antique chair for long minutes, eventually dredging herself out of an effacing daze to put the receiver back on its cradle. He's sitting there, waiting for me to phone him back, she thought, because he is weak but not evil. I need only to pick up this phone again and dial his number. I will have my husband again, and everyone else can go hang.

But what words do you use? *Mea culpa?* Father, forgive me,
I know not what I do? Just plain, I'm sorry? Hardly. If you're a
big fat fashionable horse's backside of a shaded neurotic, you say
nothing plainly. Lift the cup to this, the modern-day stratum.
Say hostile when you really mean angry. Say pass on when you
really mean die. Say intra-personal relationship when you really
mean love. Say nyet-nyet when there's si-si in your eyes. The
bogeyman's crouching over there in the corner and he'll make
you take six giant steps backward if he catches you ever saying
what you mean to say.

The ugly mantle clock, she noticed, had more to say than
anyone in town. It said ten of five. If she knew her hayseed
guest, Julia Havilland would chug up to the homestead at exactly
5:00 P.M.

Shame flushed through Marianne, Big Daddy Vodka or no
Big Daddy Vodka, and she forced herself to get to her slippered
feet and push Steve out of her mind. She shuffled through the
iniquitous house's corridors, cradling her half-filled glass, in
search of either Eunice or Mrs. Quigley.

Mrs. Quigley, whom she knew despised her, materialized,
and Marianne tried on the Steve's-shaggy-sport-shirt speech for
size.

"There'll be a Mrs. Havilland here for cocktails in ten or fifteen minutes," she directed. "Will you let her in and tell her I'll
be down presently? Serve her whatever she likes."

"Yes, ma'am." The assent was as cordial as an Eichmann nod
to a German Jew.

Upstairs, Marianne drained her drink, undressed, and
took a vigorous second shower. A vigorous shower between
drinks, one of the Culver City pansies had disclosed to her once,
impeded the flow of the strong waters to the brain. This advice
about handling the hooch was fundamentally as fraudulent as all
other advice she had received about handling the hooch, she had
discerned over the years, but the palpable fact remained that it

was physically impossible to keep drinking while you were taking a vigorous shower.

Turning off the pricking needles of the shower, Marianne stalked to the bedroom, dried herself, and selected the nubby, ebony sweater to go with the bright blood-red toreador pants. The quantities of good cologne sent up exquisite feelings of well-being in her naturally bronzed skin. In the top drawer of her accordion closet she reached for her "In-Case" fifth of brandy. She took a healthy swig, replaced it on its side behind all the pairs of shoes, closed the door, and stepped into the pants. She debated with herself about a bra, concluded the day was hot and you never matched propriety with necessity, shoved the bra back into its drawer, and brought the sweater down over her head.

The brandy had worked its wonders, on cue. The feeling of loneliness, of being intolerably alone, had lessened, was no longer excessive. Gripping her hand firmly at the top railing, she descended the long stairway, rehearsed her smile, pushed Steve and Aaron Miles and Dan Parrish into the mind's facile incinerator, and caught Julia Havilland's feverish eye.

"This isn't fair at all," Marianne complained, sweeping into the living room and taking Julia's hands. "I asked Mrs. Quigley to get you a drink the minute you arrived, and here you've been, perched on that horrid chicken crate of a couch, with nothing to do."

"That isn't so," Julia tempered, managing a smile of her own. "I just got here. I've been so busy inspecting your living room, and liking it, that I haven't thought of anything else."

"We'll remedy that in a flash," Marianne promised and called for Mrs. Quigley. She stole a fresh, furtive glance at her semi-invited guest. They had run into each other how many times before in Waymouth? Seven? Eight? She had seen Julia Havilland as a sexpot in escrow, and now, pausing for the end of the preliminaries, she questioned her original estimate. Julia Havilland was, in most respects, about as ready for Freddie as she was ready to enlist in the Foreign Legion. She would never be in danger of quibbling with Miss Rheingold for a beauty prize. But there was a manner about her that demanded attention. A look, a way of unconsciously arching an eyebrow, an unthinking method of extending an upturned palm, a nervous habit of swinging her wagon just a dot before sitting . . .

"I can't imagine what you'd find in this mortuary of a living room to hold your attention for longer than a minute," Marianne said, and was glad when Mrs. Quigley entered. "Ah, are you drinking, Julia?"

"I did ask for sherry," Julia replied.

"We're all out," Mrs. Quigley said. "I checked all through, and we're all out."

"Some Cointreau, maybe, Julia," Marianne suggested.

"Yes," Julia nodded. "Whatever that is, yes."

Mrs. Quigley glared and then disappeared.

"You'll forgive me if I help myself to my own toddy in the meantime," Marianne asserted, brushing past her on the way to the front room's portable bar. "I have it all set up here. I can talk so much better when I have the toddy in hand."

"You go right ahead," Julia directed. She wore a dark, draping dress right out of the last Marjorie Main movie. Her hair style had been fashioned by a salesman for Waring Mixers. Her long legs were gorgeous enough to be illegal.

"Here we go, podner," Marianne grinned and finished pouring. She brought her glass to the center of the room, sank happily into the armchair, sipped, and turned on her Marianne Terrin charm. "Now. What could you see in this drafty pool hall to hold your attention? If it were up to me, I'd rent all of it out to a soundstage shooting a Peter Lorre classic. If you're going to try to sell me that stuff about beauty in motion, we've had our friendship and I'm forthwith lowering you to the lions."

"Don't do that yet," Julia stressed. "I love the pictures on your walls. The Rivera. The Goya. Especially that one on the north wall."

Marianne craned her head, tightened her eyes, and again slouched. "The nude? Send me the gold ring. I done it."

"You? Truly?"

"Every pubic hair of it. A self-portrait. A result of a batch of sessions in a Waymouth adult-education class. I sat myself in front of the wall-length mirror, in the glorious raw, and just splashed paint."

"You're right. I see the resemblance now."

"You're kinder than you should be. After I finished it, I had an ineffable urge to sign at the bottom, 'Narcissistically yours, M.S.' You can see that the narcissism was so great, I didn't do it. I signed it N.H.B. Any non-nose-picking art critic will tell you that means, 'No Holds Barred'."

"You're terrible," Julia Havilland blushed.

"My talent or my morals?"

"Your talk."

"Ah, yes. And here comes Mrs. Quigley. What held you up? The friendly iceman?"

Mrs. Quigley scowled, delivered the Cointreau to Julia, and trudged back to the kitchen.

"You ought to get a load of my annointed father-in-law when he sees that picture," Marianne notified. "He shows up here in his old house every St. Swithin's Day to proffer his own make of myrrh. He takes one look at that picture, between the Goya and Rivera, and he goes absolutely loony. Maybe you've seen him. He's the soul of sixty-nine Wall Street. He sees it and remarks on its obscenity. You know: Where's the symbol of the Sistine Chapel, the Louvre, the Washington Park Exhibit?"

"I've met the type, if that helps."

"Oh, boy, a friend understands! What you can't understand is the whole picture, but that's another volume. We'll drop it."

"That isn't so. I'm listening. To everything."

Glancing at her warily, Marianne inquired, "Why?"

"Why?" Julia repeated pleasantly. "I enjoy being with you. I saw you in the movies. I hate to see volumes dropped. Shall I dip down and come up with more reasons? How many would you like?"

Marianne Sherwood dug into the dark drink she had built, eyed Julia warily, and chuckled. "You're okay, Julia," she ventured. "I guess I can stop with the checks and balances."

"Were you worried? I don't think checks and balances were indicated. Not really."

"I have a confession to make," Marianne said. "I would've said, if I'd imagined you coming on that picture, that you would have blanched and turned a dozen and a half colors and run away toward safe quarters."

"Honestly? Just from seeing a nude?"

"I had that idea."

"Then I'm the one who ought to be sorry. For seeming so backwoods. I gave up smoking a corncob pipe and feuding with the Hatfields years ago."

Marianne laughed. "I didn't mean to be insulting."

"Nor did I," Julia said, and Marianne worried that Julia lacked a sense of humor. "I doubt if I ever was more serious in my life."

There was a bashful silence for a while as each looked everywhere but at the other, and Marianne, taking delicate sips from her glass, decided they'd both agreed at the same, safe time to get onto less explosive ground. They moved from one inconsequential topic to another—how noble and overworked their respective husbands were, whether the fall season's promised shows on Broadway would be exciting or the same old tourist-aimed trash, the Sally Warner girl. One more Cointreau and two vodkas later, Marianne waited for the opportune moment to leap up and ask, "What really brought you here today?"

Julia made two or three mild acknowledgments that she might be overstaying her welcome, that Marianne doubtless had a hundred better things to do. Marianne shut one eye, peered at her wrist watch with the other, and was surprised that, for all the idle, dull chatter with this idle, dull woman, the time had sped by so fast. Certainly there were other things she could do with her time. She could go after Aaron Miles again. She could contact Dan Parrish, who surely would be in by now. She could brood about the insane way she'd behaved with Steve, maybe even gather her wisps of dignity about her and cleverly (but not too cleverly) request a rain-check for a spoiled brat who's wretchedly sorry.

And it was true that she found Julia Havilland's self-conscious thrusts at sophistication, at hopelessly and rather pitifully striving to keep up with her, a bit too heavy and cloying.

But she would not tell her to go home. The loneliness, despite the warming liquor and this morning's determined upbeat, was mossy and increasingly unutterable. And there were adjustable, if not ample, compensations in spending more time with this forlorn woman who was panting so to be a friend. The cronies in Beverly Hills and at the Bel Air parties would lift suave eyebrows, chortle, and inquire when the flower show meeting was expected to come to order. But the cronies weren't around to chortle with. Julia hadn't ever learned how to freely talk or freely think in non-flower-show terms, yet there now seemed more to her than Marianne had observed before, in town at Waymouth get-togethers, when she'd childishly gone out of her way to make her feel ill at ease.

She was trusting, guileless, unaccountably likable, but mostly trusting. She was worshipful Ole Dog Tray, but not onerously so. How often in this Sherwood-walled wilderness did you run up against a person you could wholly trust?

And all the hopeful ships had sailed out to sea by now. One more call would prod Miles' secretary to tell her to get doubly lost and for fair. Steve would have made other plans for the evening and, even if he hadn't and still was at the store waiting for a proper apology, she was afraid her brain was too scrambled to be trusted to say the key words adequately; in many areas Steve was about as sensitive as a dinosaur's belch, but lately he was able to judge she'd downed that half-drink too many long before she'd judged it herself. Dan Parrish would probably break whatever appointment he had, even at this hour, but the prospect of riding into New York just to share his bed for an hour and then riding back was a dismal one; his attention span when she simply wanted to talk was no longer than a ten-year-old boy's, and he had no benevolent interest in her outside the bed.

There was Frankie in the village, and she liked to see her now and then. But when you converged on Frankie and her stimulating gang, it usually was an all-night romp, and she wasn't up to that, either. Not this late.

"Stay and have dinner with me, Julia," she said, feeling morose and irrecoverably lost as she rose to walk stiffly across the room and make a fresh drink. "Mrs. Quigley can round up some chops and a salad and set us up on the patio."

"Oh, I wouldn't want to interfere with—"

"Goddammit!" Marianne barked, her eyes blistering at the row of whiskey bottles. "If you were going to interfere with anything, I would've told you so an hour ago and ushered you out of here. You're interfering with nothing. That prize package of a husband I was venerating before won't be home till the late, wee hours. He's discovered a young, blonde satellite and they're on the town together."

"Oh, Marianne," Julia comforted quickly and, for all Marianne knew, maybe she was being perfectly sincere. "I'm so sorry. I didn't know … "

"Nothing for you to be sorry about. You're a lucky girl, Julia. You know where your husband is every minute. We love to call ourselves so teddibly urbane around these Evers Drive parts and say we don't give a hang who our men're spending their evenings with, but you know what that's a heaping bucket of."

Chuckling without a hint of mirth, she grabbed the neck of the bottle and was embarrassed to detect that she'd made a slight lurch. She glanced swiftly to see if Julia, whose face of sympathy was almost vocal, had detected it, too; she hated to seem like a messy drunk in front of anyone, particularly someone it was momentarily important to impress. No, Julia's expression was too wrapped up in condolence. Not that it much mattered. Julia Havilland would stay with her, fried or not fried.

And I feel this dungeony day like getting classically fried, she thought, so in the bag that the next time I visualize Mrs. Quigley squealing to Steve about his misbehaving wife, I'll be able to laugh them both out of my spindly consciousness.

"Come on," Marianne offered. "Bring your Cointreau bottle and glass. The patio's thataway, through that room and straight ahead. I'll be out in half a sec. You can look out and see your street, Northrop, from there. Did you know that?"

"Honestly?" Julia asked in a suddenly troubled voice.

She watched Julia walk with Wac colonel carriage and thought slyly, Those legs of hers look as smooth as cream. I wonder if she'd yell for the sheriff if I told her so?

The evening had turned cool, but that was no reason to go inside. Music from the hi-fi had been piped outside and the lulling quality of an old Sarah Vaughan record was pleasant as they sat on the patio and leisurely sipped from their drinks. The dinner had been finished long ago and Marianne had kept on drinking, although she had privately chosen to take it easy. Julia, who seldom drank more than ten drinks a year, had had two cups of coffee after dinner and had explained she was content. Ever so gently, Marianne had forced another brandy on her and, when that was done, had proffered still another so unnoticeably that Julia had accepted it without a fuss.

"It's all some sort of gremlin hodgepodge and you'll see soon enough how mistaken you are," Julia was saying, after Marianne talked for longer than she'd expected about Steve and his playing around with any young chick who blinked her saccharine eyes in his direction. She had no idea why she'd wilfully invited Julia along for this red-herring ride.

"Mistaken, my sainted behind," Marianne disparaged, frowning straight ahead. "If I said that the woods were burning if the woods were burning, would I be mistaken? Ah, let's leave it lay, honey. I didn't mean to bring you up on the latest chapter of Love's Labours Lost. You have your own troubles."

"Troubles? Who said I have troubles?"

"I said," Marianne asserted riskily. "We're old pals by now. When you're ready, you may tell me why you decided to phone me and come to see me today."

"Honestly, Marianne, I don't know what you mean."

She stretched pleasurably. "Oh, I talk too much, I guess. I tend to talk in second-act-curtain lines. Steve told me that just today, and he's right. What I meant, honey, was that nobody's problems ever touch anyone else's, and that, as far as I can see, is only as it should be. My marriage smells on ice and yours is just about flawless. You can listen to me blather with hoary tales about adultery—that's hoary without the 'w'—and you can sympathize as a friend forever, but only up to a point. Unless your husband is making time with the upstairs maids of the land, and if you know he is, you can give me that third ear only so long. It's only natural," she shrugged. "What the hell."

"I wouldn't exactly call you the easiest person in the world to understand," Julia submitted.

"Which reminds me. In a few days I will get on my horse and ride over to be interviewed by the Alders folks. If *you* think I'm hard to understand, they'll quite possibly scratch their heads and have me locked up."

"You really volunteered for that survey?"

"I said I did, didn't I? You volunteered, too, didn't you? I would've imagined you'd be right there at the head of the line. You know: the holy seriousness of the inexorable march of science. You go for culture and man's thirst for knowledge and all that."

"Oh, no, I'd never volunteer."

"Good Lawdy, why not? They don't fingerprint you."

"I— Well, Evelyn Pendleton called me a number of times and tried to browbeat me into it—for the sake of science, as you said. But I have certain reservations about it, although I'm no prude. It's—well, it's like being naked, and not even on one's own terms. You know."

"You keep saying 'You know'," Marianne said bluntly. "I don't know anything you don't tell me."

Derailed, Julia pressed, "What I mean is that a woman shouldn't be browbeaten into telling everything that's intimate about herself."

"You say you're not a prude. I differ. I've come to like you a lot, so I can make this observation. Julia, you are a prude."

Julia looked up sharply, as though she'd been smacked.

"A thought occurred to me when you said 'naked'," Marianne declared, in a purposely offhand tone, and hoped that she wasn't going too far with this pathetically egoless woman. "It ought to be fun to do a nude painting of you. I'm not about to step into Picasso's size twelves, but I've won a few dinky awards around here with my oils. Would you be interested?"

"You're teasing me."

"Now that's about the most circuitous answer I've heard since—well, tonight," Marianne remarked. Julia was so obviously uncomfortable in her striped, narrow patio chair that Marianne felt a tinge of regret for having thought the cat-and-mouse game would make either of them happy.

"You—must admit, Marianne," Julia mildly reproved, nervously cupping her brandy, her voice strained, "you're not the type of person I meet every day in the week. You're a little — frank in the way you talk."

Marianne sat forward long enough to freshen her glass and saw, with only fleeting alarm, that she'd nearly killed the fifth, even though she recalled having promised herself to space her drinks. She was hitting it pretty hard lately, as Steve preached to her, but one thing pleased her. Her words, however senseless, weren't running together.

"Frank? Maybe so. But I'll tell you something, honey. I used to listen to the radio when I was a kid and I came home from school. I'd hear Little Orphan Annie. If you sent them an Ovaltine wrapper they'd sent you a milk glass that wouldn't break when you dropped it. Do you remember what her dog used to say, whatever his name was?"

"Sandy."

"Yeah, Sandy. He used to say something."

" 'Arf'."

" 'Arf'."

" 'Arf'," Marianne nodded. "And I decided something one hell of a long time ago. You know what? I decided, that's a lot more than most of us ever say in a lifetime."

"Marianne, help me to know you better. Everyone has a philosophy. You seem to work so hard to sound so cynical, but I'm sure it isn't truly you."

"How're you so sure?"

"Because I am. Past the cynicism, what do you believe in?"

"Um. Let's see. Hedonism. Good, clear, old-fashioned hedonism. I like to drink great quantities and I like to have sex with people who appeal to me." She paused and, because there was silence, peered at Julia. "What's wrong? Does that startle you as a philosophy? You asked me and I told you. I live to enjoy myself, period, no tortured psyche, and if you can come up with a better philosophy, I'll curtsey reverently."

"I can't agree with you. And I don't believe you do, either."

"Okay, give me a better one. Give me yours."

"I believe in the responsibility," Julia replied rigidly, "of leaving this world in just a little better condition than when I first found it."

"Bushwah," Marianne snickered, and rose to her feet with agreeable litheness. "I love you to pieces, honey, but bush-wah."

"How can you act that way?" Julia scolded and Marianne, strolling within a six-foot radius near the striped chair, was amused to see that her adoring empathizer was getting a little sore. "If you don't mind my saying so—and I'd never dream of speaking this personally if it weren't for those brandies I had—your language is like a, well, a juvenile delinquent's. And if I didn't have my wits about me, I'd think that you actually believed half of those disreputable things you were saying. But I know differently. You're a good and fine and decent person. You say what you say merely to shock. What I can't understand is why you feel you need to shock."

"Have you completed your character analysis?" Marianne asked fondly, standing close to the chair, smiling affectionately.

"I—suppose so."

"I'm not out to shock anybody, honey, certainly not you. If you choose to get shocked, though, you wouldn't want to blame me, would you?"

"Oh, I didn't say you shocked *me*. I've already explained that, despite anything anyone may say about me, I'm not a prude."

Marianne snickered, still standing close and swiftly unnerving her. The hi-fi was playing a soupy, flagrantly inappropriate waltz. It was clear that the poor girl wanted nothing so much as to free herself from the confining chair, but if she did she would have come face to face with her hostess, and there would be no immediately escapable distance between them.

"Then answer me something, honey," Marianne baited, still affectionate. "I invited you to pose for me in the buff. I'll admit I maybe sidetracked you there with the way I sometimes ramble, but you didn't go for the invitation at all. I saw your face, I saw the way that back arched when I repeated your word 'naked'. Your word, mind, not mine."

"You were reading things into—"

"You don't shock easily and you're not a prude. Well, what was wrong with my offer if *you* weren't reading things into it? Lewd things, dirty things, things I didn't mean at all. When you came here—"

"Please," Julia murmured.

"—today you looked at my painting on the living-room wall and you saw it as art. Puny art, maybe, because God knows I'm far from a major painter, but as art, nevertheless. Healthy and free."

"Marianne," Julia lamented softly, unendurably trapped, "for some strange reason, you're suddenly riding me. You sound angry, almost hateful. It isn't necessary. Why are you doing it?"

"You're not a prude? I was no juvenile delinquent when I asked to paint you. Why didn't you meet my eyes and give me a simple yes or no? You're not meeting my eyes, even now. Why did you say, 'You're teasing'? That's how you answered. Where's the discrepancy? Why did you say that?"

The soupy waltz had ended and so, too, Marianne sensed, had her thoroughly unwarranted tirade. Night had come. Mrs. Quigley's bedroom window, perceptible from the patio, was lighted. The pause was melancholy and haunting.

"Because," Julia breathed, scarcely above a whisper, sitting mournfully at the end of her chair, staring at the brick floor and punctuating each word as if she required time to examine each word, "because there are many reasons. Because I'm not used to conversation. Because I'm a little frightened of you. Because I'm a long and lanky stick of a woman. Because I am homely.

Because—" She sighed and brought herself with tired, sexless finality out of the chair. She was on a level with Marianne's eyes and her expression, stronger and more confident now than Marianne had ever witnessed it, dared renewed baiting.

"What is it, Julia?" Marianne asked.

"You were rude."

"I know I was," Marianne agreed tenderly. "I'm getting drunk as a coot and I say awful things when I start getting drunk. Does that help in any way, honey?"

"Does it help? That's one of the million things I don't know. I think the thing I envy you most for is that you never appear confused, especially when you're most confused of all. Marianne, I'd better go home now."

"Why now?"

"It's late."

"Why this minute?"

Julia was no longer afraid to reach her eyes. "I don't handle my confusion as well as you do. I started to see only a moment or so ago why I did come to see you. You asked me why before, but I didn't know. Now I think I'm beginning to. Those drinks you served me are sending spirals through my head, and they're making me feel terrible, and I have just reason enough now not to talk any more." She extended her hand. "Good night, Marianne."

"Now who's being disconnected in the way she talks?"

"I am," Julia nodded, without a smile. "Please don't make me talk any more. That last brandy has just got to me and I feel dreadfully ashamed."

"How will you be about getting home?"

"I'll be fine. I have the car keys right here."

Marianne kissed her cheek. Julia jumped, as if bitten, far out of proportion to what the innocent kiss had intended. She forced a vacant smile, and then ramrodded a walk to her Chevrolet.

The phone call came twenty-five minutes later, after Marianne had ascended the wide stairs to her bedroom.

"Are you anxious to know something?" the voice inquired.

"What?"

"I'm tight on those brandies."

"Oh?"

"And there's something else, but be sure you don't ever make me repeat it ever again."

"What?"

"I have the suspicion I'm in love."

The receiver was fumblingly replaced.

On the second floor of the creaky, winter-drafty Sherwood house, most of Steve's effects could be seen with the least of trouble. Marianne thought back to the good days, the times when marriage with Steven Sherwood had given gold-plated guarantees of substantial, permanent success. Forcing herself to dissolve all greasy thoughts of Julia Havilland, she sat at her upstairs desk and dialed Dan Parrish's number in the city.

A strange voice, a woman's voice said, "Yes?"

"Maybe I have the wrong number," Marianne conceded. "I'm calling Mr. Parrish's residence."

"Who's calling him?" questioned the voice, snipped from the sound track of an old Toby Wing movie.

" ... Marianne."

"Uh huh. You hold tight, and I see'f he's in."

The desperate wait didn't need to take this long, surely. She could hear voices, argumentative voices, tell-her-nobody's-home voices, and all at once one of those querulous voices belonged to Dan, her mustached and seductive Dan, and he was being furtively hoarse in the background about an old bag who was demented and always on his tail.

It's Frankenstein night, she thought, and hung up.

Smoking a cigarette, cornering a forefinger at her chin and tapping her cheek with her thumb, Marianne rocked from one foot to the other and back again, feeling the liquor but not as distinctly as she believed she should have, and rewelcomed the return of the jitters. Almost before she knew it, she would be seated at her appointment with that Alders man—the card said his name was either Crayne or Cayne—and every confidence would be respected. If she wanted to talk out all that was in her at this minute, Crayne or Cayne would not stop her, and Crayne or Cayne would not censure.

I need help, Crayne or Cayne, she announced in her bedroom, and to hell with whether the Eunices or the Mrs. Quigleys or the Julia Havillands could hear her. I am a foul, rotten mess of a woman, and if you're the gentleman and scholar I assume you are, will you kindly tell me why I'm so gogo in the skull that I become overly moralistic only when I'm overly crocked?

The appointment was for eleven o'clock sharp, two days away. It was too far away. Marianne lowered her hand, staggered to the bed which was familiar, the bed Mrs. Quigley had turned down for her, and let the hesitancies pingpong through her head. Dashing out her cigarette and lighting another, she could see Steve. He was sitting in orchestra seats with the bustiest of blondes, not a stroke over nineteen, and they were applauding the Merman show. At the final curtain he would taxi her home, let her femininely pour him some Nescafe in her grimy walkup, and he would complain about his home life. She would lispingly excuse herself and return, after a long rash of running her bathroom sink faucets, in one of those Mandarin housecoats. She would keep lisping. She would remain shrewdly stupid. The housecoat would somehow open unexpectedly at inoperable times, and they both would make somber, abject apologies. She would accidentally locate Rupert Brooke poetry in her bookcase and would ask if he'd mind reading it aloud in his musical baritone as she made herself comfy on the other daybed. He would clear his throat and commence reading, but by the fourth page her middle button, the vital button, would without announcement pop off and this would make her pout. He would close her book to comfort her. There would be the superabundant yet unshed tears, and the overplay of Sinatra records, and a noise-less clap of lusty thunder, and he would dry her tearless tears by picking her up and carrying her to the right bed, as he had seen it done in a George Brent movie. . . .

Staggering, Marianne felt the old-new queasiness in her belly, the warning that it was time to reach up for the light and fall to sleep, but she was not about to give in yet. Not on this crud-ridden, woefully hapless day. She made her way to the accordion closet and brought the "In-Case" brandy bottle down. It felt refreshingly cool to the hand. Uncapping it, she poured two balky fingers worth into the hidden glass, drank without stop, and sighted the telephone. She cocked her head for a fresh cigarette and, after a moment of confusion—someone once had kissed her and told her she never appeared confused, especially when she was most confused of all, whatever that meant—spied a whole unopened pack on the table nearest her. She lighted one and, sitting on the neat bed, stooped for the Manhattan directory and slapped her fingers through it until she came to the number of The Plaza.

"Yes. Hello, Miss Terrin," Aaron Miles' secretary greeted in a cheery voice.

"You know me now."

"I do indeed."

"Get me Mr. Miles."

"He is not in."

"You never told me your name. What's your name?"

"Miss Washburn."

"Miss Washburn," Marianne repeated. "Tell me something, Miss Washburn. Did we meet on a War Bond Tour? Did I do something to you you didn't like? Is there something that puts you against me?"

"Why, not at all, Miss Terrin."

"Get me Mr. Miles."

"I've told you several times, Miss Terrin, he isn't—"

"You miserable grinning bitch, you get him on the line or I'll find you and kick out all your buck teeth. I'm here in my study with a high-powered microscope, gazing at you, and I know you have buck teeth."

"There are other calls waiting—"

"You Goddamn rotten son of a bitch!" Marianne cried, standing and spitting out a stream of oaths she hadn't remembered using since she was a kid. "I'm Marianne Terrin! Do you need that spelled for you, out there in your crummy, chromy office? You trek on out here and I'll show you scrapbook on scrapbook. Considine, Conniff, Earl Wilson, Leonard Lyons, Sobol, Winchell, Hedda Hopper, all of 'em, you name 'em, I got 'em. Don't slough me off, you ninety-dollar-a-week nothing! I'm Terrin! You get me Miles or—"

And then: "Or?"

"Please. I have a way of talking I know isn't always nice."

"Phone the City Dump, Miss Terrin. You'll never get on this line again."

She caught sight of herself in the full-length mirror after she cried, "Hello? Hello?" too often into the receiver. Throughout the whole freaky day she had struck out, and yet she still looked like nine million dollars. Love? Love, hell. If you worked it right, you could be loved, and without Miss Washburn-type proof demands. Marianne went back to the side of the bed, gritting her teeth, and pulled her address book from between a stack of *New Yorkers,* the ones which should have been put in the garbage weeks ago. She frowningly read the address over and over until she was sure she had memorized it, and then closed the book. She descended the back stairs, jiggling the car keys, and slid into the Thunderbird. The Fiat was missing from the garage. That had to mean Steve was in his symbolic white tie and tails tonight and was doing nicely with that lisping Manhattan girl.

The night was clear, but the drive to Northrop Avenue seemed to take forever. She drove up to the address, which was dark except for one small light on the second floor, but carefully maneuvered the Thunderbird ahead for at least another half-block before she parked. She walked back, with vigilant caution, to the house and rang the front-door bell. It was necessary to ring five times before she saw a hall light switch on and Julia, in a Twelfth-Century nightgown peek out and open the door.

"Marianne!"

"Ask me in?"

"Come in!"

The door closed and bolted behind them.

"You have a fine, solid, old house here, Julia."

"You're—how did you make it, Marianne? Are you all right?"

Tapping the edge of her nose, Marianne winked. "Best shape ever. And speaking of best shape, you got nothing to be guilty about, either."

"Let me heat some coffee."

"You sleeping? I wake you up?"

Julia was busy turning off strategic lights, the ones the neighbors would see. "Not quite."

"Sorry."

"I'll get the coffee going."

"You still tight on the brandies, Julia?"

"Oh. No."

"I'm still tight on mine."

"I can—see that. That's why I say: Let me get the coffee."

"Can you forget the coffee?"

"Marianne…"

" 'Marianne' what?"

"It's been an odd day."

"You say the word, Julia, and I'll curtsey reverently and go home."

"I didn't say that."

"You shouldn't wear librarian nightgowns like that, Julia. If your gorgeous legs're any indication, you should wear nothing but gossamer silk. I said it. You have gorgeous legs. I wanted to say it all day long."

"Marianne," Julia pleaded in the semi-dark of the foyer, "I just don't know how to answer you."

"Somebody phoned me a little while ago on the telephone and said something about being in love."

"I was being school-girl silly. The brandies hadn't worn off."

"Julia, be a friend. Don't embarrass me. I don't want coffee, I don't want Sunday-school lectures. I don't want to stagger around here in your lonely foyer. Do one of two things. Order me to go back home, or invite me in and ask me to stay. One or the other."

"Marianne..."

"One or the other, dear."

"Stay, Marianne."

Somehow, on the wobbliest of knees, she was guided upstairs and into a too-huge bedroom with rich, ancient chiffoniers and twin beds. She was aware of the overlight being snuffed and of Julia's terror. She wasn't entirely sure of how her clothes came off or how she reached the bed. At one point she goggled through heavy lids and blinked at the loveliest body she had ever seen.

"Tell the truth," Marianne demanded. "Did you expect me?"

"No."

"Sorry I came?"

"Not now."

"Tomorrow?"

"Tomorrow, yes."

"Tell me something. Why'd you call me and come to see me today?"

"For this," Julia replied.

"Whyn't you say that sooner?"

"Shhh, darling. Sleep now. Sleep, my darling."

CHAPTER FOUR

❧ ❧ ❧

I N ROOM 431, Nelson Partridge sat across from the tall, well-groomed but unimaginatively dressed woman and listened to her unrequested defense of her private life. If she's so in favor of the dignity of concealment and privacy, he thought, what the devil is she doing here?

Nelson continued to give his supportive nod but turned the inner volume as she spoke. Surreptitiously he checked his notes. Mrs. Julia Buckley Havilland. 38 years old. Husband a realtor and insurance broker. Married 15 years this Thanksgiving. No children. Happily married and ideally suited to each other (*this intelligence repeated proudly and a little desperately four times within the first thirty-five minutes'*). Slight nervous tic just above right unplucked eyebrow.

A virgin prior to marriage? Certainly. And if he wanted to know the statistical truth, country-wide surveys or no country-wide surveys, the vast majority of young women brought up with care and taste retained their virtue until their wedding nights. Only a handful of immature misfits, you know, still believe we're descended from the apes.

Petting prior to marriage? Of course not. Oh, there were boys in high school and at Gerrick College, which she attended (*Major: English literature; high honors throughout her four years there*) who occasionally attempted to get out of hand. But she had learned early and accurately from her mother that a young man's good or bad behavior is invariably guided by the manner in which a girl comports herself. She had kept that advice uppermost in her mind, and she had delighted in her husband's pleasure that she had come to her marriage unsoiled.

"These stories about decent girls losing their sense of values just because they're in college away from home are highly overstated," she upbraided Nelson at one point during the session, as though he were interested in arguing with her. "Speaking for myself, I know I had more elevating things than sex on my mind while I was a student at Gerrick."

"Such as what, Mrs. Havilland?"

"The more healthful, the more aesthetic life, for instance," she replied stiffly, and he wondered what either of them had said to bring such a suffusive blush to her cheeks. "I found enough romance in the pursuit of poetry. I was extremely lucky in my third year at Gerrick. I took a course in Elizabethan poetry with Mona Vancini, who was teaching there that year. If you don't know anything about poetry, this wouldn't mean anything to you, but Mona Vancini went on to become one of our finest poets.

"We weren't merely instructor and student," she continued. "The years have raced by and I haven't seen her since she became famous, but I still cherish her as the dearest friend I ever had. That was a rewarding, thrilling time. I'll grant you there might have been some girls during that period who were wild, and went off to grubby backroad motels and all with boys, but they couldn't possibly have been given what I was given—culture, intellectual curiosity and enrichment, uplift." She paused. "That, Dr. Partridge, is how I spent my 'wild' time before I graduated and married Mr. Havilland. I rejected sex for something infinitely greater. When the mind is filled with the wonders of beautiful language, and the soul is fed with the wonders of the pure friendships, there is never the need to entertain thoughts of the illicit."

Suavely forcing her to meet his eyes, Nelson said, "As a matter of fact, Mrs. Havilland, I know Mona Vancini's work. I'm no authority on her poetry, but I've read some of it. I've seen her photographs and read about her, too."

"That's—very interesting," she said lamely, and he observed that she was eager to change the subject.

As she sat restlessly in her hardbacked chair and told him about her normal, perfectly wonderful parents, he was firmly convinced he had got to her, that he had subtly rocked her self-righteous, stodgy boat. Mona Vancini was an adept but sadly minor poetess, unknown to most audiences. The thimbleful of readers who read her woolly, esoteric work, or who knew the mildest vital statistics about her, knew she was a practicing lesbian, and frequently a noisy one, at that.

"—and my mother worked, so that she wasn't at home as often as she would have liked, but we had one memorable, unswerving tradition in our home on Chatsworth Boulevard. Three evenings a week, rain or shine, my parents and my brother Buddy and I met at the living-room piano and had a rousing, old-fashioned community sing. My parents held the belief, and I agree with it, that a family who sings together—"

She took the time to mention Mona Vancini by name, Nelson thought, as if she expressly hoped I'd know the name and the connotation. And maybe that's exactly why the sober Mrs. Havilland, with all her overworked sexlessness, is here today. She wanted to change the subject. But she didn't want to change the subject. She's the classic example of repressed or dormant homosexuality, and in her stumbling, Nob Hilltype way she's asking me to give her the go-ahead signal.

For a short while Nelson allowed her to waste both their time with her rambling and strikingly unimportant tales about the superiority of the aesthetic life. When the hour was nearly up, and when he was thoroughly convinced that she was apprehensively waiting for him to guide her, he let her finish a sentence and then called her obviously divided attention to the papers and pen in front of him.

"Intercourse with someone other than your husband since marriage?" he inquired perfunctorily, pen poised.

"Adultery? You couldn't have been listening to me during this interview, Dr. Partridge."

"I assure you, Mrs. Havilland, I've heard every word."

"I'd call the question impudent if I weren't satisfied with your Institute's objectivity," she rebuked, sitting up a trifle straighter. "Since I married Mr. Havilland, I haven't looked at another man."

"I said 'someone,' Mrs. Havilland," Nelson maintained with a brief smile. "I didn't say a man, necessarily."

Her eyes became rounder with what she had every right to deem an insult, considering the steadfast quality of innocence she had been showing, but there wasn't the hint of a sign that she was about to rustle her feathers and stomp out of this room.

Not just yet.

"That question was totally uncalled for, Doctor," she scolded, in an unfamiliar voice which guaranteed him he'd struck the poignant nerve, "and I think you know it. You're presumably a young man of character. One would imagine that with those assets you'd be able to merely look at me and judge I'm not a—well, what would the word be? A pervert."

"Why does that question upset you so much, Mrs. Havilland? Why not the other questions about relations before marriage, the sex practices and frequency of relations with your husband? Why this one?"

"I don't know that I'm appreciably more upset by—"

"But you are," he declared quietly.

"You're talking, Doctor, about a practice which shames and disgusts me. The thought of it shames and disgusts me. It's the province of sick animals."

"Let me submit, Mrs. Havilland, that your information is mistaken," Nelson stated blandly. "Our careful statistics show us

that homosexual interludes, even long-range affairs, among educated, tasteful married women are far from rare. They do appear
to be rare among the lower class, lower-income group, but not
among the upper-middle class."

"That hardly concerns me," she answered stiffly.

"Be that as it may, and whether or not you view the experience as sick and perverted, it's one which evidently enriches the
lives of a considerable number of adult and discriminating married women."

"Why are you telling me this?" she pressed, her frown stern.

Shrugging, Nelson smiled again and turned his palms
upward. "It's as I've told you. Your information about a particular facet of life is mistaken. The Alders Institute has only two
missions: to banish ignorance by learning how people conduct
themselves sexually and then edifying as many other people as
possible."

"This—bisexuality...Do you condone such behavior?"

"It's not the Alders Institute's function to condone or con-
demn; not at this time. We are preparing several chapters on
bisexuality, though, in our next book. If it's of interest to you,
we expect to conclude that the experience, when practiced by
mature people who can handle societal guilt, is neither harmful
nor unusual, that in fact it can be amply rewarding."

The news hit her, Nelson was sure, right between her wor-
riedly acquisitive eyes. Reaching for the props of her purse and
white summer gloves, she volunteered, "I see that our time is just
about up, Doctor." She stood regally from the chair and Nelson
rose with her, no longer interested in keeping her. "I trust I
haven't been too argumentative."

"Not at all."

"And that—whatever we discussed can help your rather odd
statistics in some small way."

"It can, indeed. Ah—when we interview a subject who has
been unusually interesting, Mrs. Havilland, we invite her back

for one or more sessions before we leave town. If you would care to come again, I believe I can fit you in to another hour. Perhaps at a more convenient time of day."

"No, thank you, Dr. Partridge," she dissented politely. "At the risk of sounding rude, I'll have to confess that your survey probably will find me more interesting than I find your survey. Good day."

"Good day, Mrs. Havilland. Thank you for coming."

Nelson jotted the notes on Mrs. Julia Buckley Havilland, the ones Phil Morrow would want to hear, in a swift shorthand. He sat back, laced his beautiful, delicate fingers behind his head, and waited for the next interviewee to be shown in.

These were the sessions that made the whole obscene thing worthwhile. He hadn't the foggiest doubt that he'd told her precisely what she'd come to hear.

There was always the paltry, largely groundless fear that he just mightn't have brought the door of her consciousness ajar at the psychologically crucial moment, that she would try to eradicate her guilt feelings by spilling the beans. Conceivably she could rear up and repeat what he knew perfectly well was hogwash to some responsive party—such as Morrow—and the job he wanted to keep would be at an end.

But then there had been the fear before, in the other towns, the other cities, and nothing had come of it. The egoless little ciphers had stalked or tiptoed into the room he occupied. In time he'd been able to listen to them for only a few minutes and recognize them as latent inverts. Suavely, always indirectly, he'd opened the dark door just a tempting trace, just enough to make them see for themselves what truths they had feared to see. No one could accuse him of taking these innocent clods by the hand and leading them down the pervert's primrose path. If he'd stepped on sore toes that didn't want to be stepped on, then why hadn't there been a rash of complaints? Or even one?

At a timid knock on the door, he called, "Yes. Come in." A clean-cut boy of seventeen or eighteen, wearing a severe crewcut and a leviathan *W* on his sweater entered. Nelson remembered the card. This would be Warren Pendleton. When Morrow had asked Waymouth parents to permit their teen-age children to volunteer, the minister who'd worked helpfully ahead of time with Herb Graham had been the town's first citizen to offer his son to the lion's den.

"Dr. Partridge?"

"That's right. You're Warren Pendleton." They shook hands. "Sit down here, won't you? Say, that's a snappy crew-cut you have there. I always wanted one, but I never had the nerve to tell the barber."

Julia emerged onto inactive Chancellor Street from the building's side door, the same one she'd used when she'd entered the building an hour ago. The last thing she wished to have happen—well, one of the last—was for Charles or any of Charles' business associates or friends to learn she had been here. She had received an early appointment when she'd telephoned for one. She had made them promise that only the person who took the message and the psychologist she would meet would know her name, that otherwise it was to be kept inviolately secret. As far as she could surmise, they had respected her wish.

If she had left by one of the building's front doors five minutes before, she would have seen Marianne Sherwood, bustling to make her own appointment on time.

Once on Mercantile Avenue, which joined Griffin, she took a deep breath and felt better. Any of the girls, or Charles' acquaintances, or even Charles himself who had flown back from Spokane this morning, could catch sight of her from here on in and not think anything out of the way. She was shopping, and that was that. She was relieved that she had had the good sense to park the telltale Chevrolet in Chance Murray's lot adjoining the tearoom, and had walked the side streets to the building. Unless Dr. Partridge or the person who took the telephone message elected to broadcast her appearance, she had spent the day at Sherwoods and the other stores.

"Ho there, Julia!" she heard and turned to meet Helen Corbett, waddling toward her with that tigerish gap-toothed grin of hers. She remembered the abstracted yet palatial loneliness which had made her only last Saturday afternoon call the numbers of Helen and the other Helens, the colossal bores she hadn't wanted to be with in the first place.

Only last Saturday. A shored eternity ago.

"You look like you're chasing around like a chicken without a head," Helen charged amiably. "I hooted twice before you heard me.

"Forgive me, Helen," she said and glanced about her to detect whether she recognized anyone else. "My mind was scattered all over."

"You're not feverish, are you? You look red's an apple."

"I'm in fine condition. Ah—what're you doing up in these parts, Helen? I think of you as just about never leaving Northrop Avenue."

"Big sale on at Weaver's," Helen notified in her anticipated clipped tones. "Why're *you* here? On your way to tell that cage of sex fiends all the dirt?" She guffawed, as Julia imagined she would.

"You put your finger on it. I'm just the one to tell it, too. I—ah—read about the Weaver sale and I thought I'd peek in. But they were crowded, so I peeked out."

"Crowded? Not Weaver's. That ad in *The Spectator* didn't draw flies, Peggy Fowler told me. I was there for an hour and they didn't draw flies."

"Oh? Well, I was wrong. Anyway, I'm on my way back home."

"Have a soda with me," Helen said. "It's a hot day."

"Next time, Helen, all right? Charles just flew back this morning from Washington State and I want to be home when he gets back from his office."

"Sure. Let's stay in touch."

At the bottom of the Waymouth Hill, Julia stepped into Arvin's for a glass of iced tea and was happy, for the very first time since she could recall, to be completely alone.

"It's so nice to see you again, Mrs. Havilland," greeted Miss Efflinger, the ancient hostess who would have been lost without her menus.

"And it's nice to see you, too, Miss Efflinger," Julia nodded as she glided to the booth in the room's direct center.

After Katrin took her order and provided her usual obeisant nod (how queer, thought Julia, that Katrin Halversen and I went to Waymouth High together and she feels she has to be this reverently distant), Julia thought about that young Dr. Partridge, and decided that "impudent" was indeed the right word to describe him. She had behaved with unwinking, almost majestic dignity, but he had assumed that something about a dignified woman's presence should impel him to offer her his statistics about the shaded interests of women.

How had he classified them? Educated, mature, tasteful women.

She'd asked for no such information. What he'd volunteered had surely answered most of the cheerless, tantalizing questions she had been asking herself, but that far from excused his impudence.

Had he had the glimmer of a notion, when she'd mentioned Mona Vancini's name, that she and Mona had loved one another? For an indecisive moment in that airless room with him, she had had the deliriously causeless fantasy that he and Mona had met (after all, he traveled all around the country, and he did know, apparently, who Mona was), and that Mona had proudly rejoiced that she and Julia Buckley had known each other, deeply.

How, she thought, would I possibly have dealt with that if he'd known everything and could have delivered chapter and verse?

The iced tea came. Katrin remained for a moment to chat about her twin sister Jana's new job with the Government and about her mother, who'd broken a hip last month on her 75th birthday but who soon would be as good as new. Julia listened courteously, hiding her impatience. Katrin probably would go home tonight and cheer up her mother by saying she'd seen that dishwater-dowdy Julia Buckley at the tearoom. She would add something like, "She'll never change, that one. I'll bet she still writes letters to Santa Claus." The mother would scold, "Now hush. She's a decent, refined person. The world would be a better place to live in if more people were like her."

When Katrin left the booth, Julia sipped at the tea but found she was too giddy to stay. Paying her check, she crossed the street to Chance Murray's lot and drove home. Marianne hadn't called her yesterday, and she had been hesitant to call Marianne. Maybe there would be a message for her when she reached the house. If not, she would wait another hour or so and then make the call.

Charles was tired from his trip and likely wouldn't budge from the living room tonight, but that would present no problem. She would say she wanted to drop in on a friend, and he wouldn't put up an argument.

I am finally come alive, thought Julia. I will be happy if Charles never touches me again.

There was always at least one Mrs. Steven Sherwood type in each community, Mike Crayne thought, and this one across from him, in the frequently lusty way she talked, even in her physical makeup, filled the expected bill. What separated her from the rest of the classy yet jadedly avowed wildcats was that her husband belonged to a conspicuously prominent family.

As their session passed the halfway mark and she continued to gladly recount her history of bed gymnastics, Mike scanned his notes. 35 years old. Apparently working at neither acting career nor marriage. Engagingly attractive and vividly aware of it. Clever with her defenses, indicating she'd had long practice at delivering pre-censored intimate statements about self on cue. Supplies three overly breezy justifications for hedonism (uses word hedonism often, always with smile): 1—her husband not faithful, so why should she be?; 2—background of flagrantly immoral, disinterested mother; 3—"Only on earth so long, anyway, so why let worms have it?"

"Let's talk a bit more about your mother," Mike suggested, taking great care to show in no way that she attracted him except for the purposes of the survey. She chain smoked and took deep, relishing puffs. Her white dress was extremely kind to her fine figure, but not garishly so. In another time, another place, at a fashionable bar, say, he saw himself accidentally seated next to her. He saw her signify, with a slight but provocative lift of the eyebrow, that she wouldn't be impossible to escort upstairs. He hoped to God he would have the stamina to invite her to get lost. She was every smart man's image of immeasurable trouble.

"My mother?" she repeated congenially. "You really like to dig deep, don't you?"

"Let's talk about her."

Mrs. Sherwood helped herself to another cup of coffee at the little table beside her. "There's no raving chance she'll ever be elected Mother of the Year—although I understand she's discovered religion in the last few years, so maybe that'll do the trick. She was a waitress at one of those subterranean honky-tonks in Albion, Texas." Mrs. Sherwood looked at him evenly. "That's a euphemism, Dr. Crayne. When translated, it means she was a part-time hooker. She'd stopped being pretty in her middle twenties, but that didn't seem to hurt business. She was one of the most enterprising hustlers in that rotten dust-bowl town I grew up in."

"You know for a fact what she was?"

"Do you know for a fact that your mother was a good woman and obeyed the law?" she snapped. "Then I know for a fact what my mo-thaw was. My father—I'll give him the benefit of the doubt and call him my father—took one of those famous southwest Big Man powders a year after I was born. Until I left the old homestead—the old homestead is another euphemism, meaning a rat-infested five-flight walkup in the cutthroat part of town—she'd stagger home with one husband after another. The queer thing is that some of them honestly were lawful husbands. I once added up the score and came to the conclusion that by the time I was thirteen I had eight stepfathers. Four of them I was sure of. I had a broom-closet room directly next to hers. There were plenty more nights than I can remember when I'd lie on my lumpy cot and listen to the symphony. The bottles dropping and the glasses clinking. The loud, drunko arguments with enough of the basic words to scald a sailor's parrot. And the squeaky springs, and the huffing and puffing, like a couple of tired but belligerent bison."

"When did you leave home?" Mike asked.

She chuckled and blandly picked a tiny piece of cigarette paper from her lower lip. "Let's say I shamed the family honor and *had* to leave. Did you ever see that marvelous cartoon, Doctor, about the beatnik mother and father gazing with horror at their small son? He's wearing a baseball uniform and the mother says, 'Little League? My God, darling, where have we failed you?' "

Mike laughed.

"You'd think that's the sort of thing that would upset the old girl back home, wouldn't you? No, sir. I would expect that in your vast experience, Dr. Crayne, you've come across the term 'gang bang.' And," she added saucily, "maybe even taken a creative role in one."

"I know the term."

"Well, I was the group leader of one, at the acned age of fourteen. I've read most of the sober psychology textbooks, so don't prod me about how I think it contributed to the souped-up events that followed it. You know damned well, and I know damned well, too.

"It was one of my better improvisations," she went on. "Spur of the moment, or nearly spur of the moment. A boy scratched like a chicken, as we used to say at the Sorbonne, and when I said okay, he asked if a friend of his could watch. What the hell. I told him to bring all the kids on the block who could keep their mouths shut.

"Naturally, the production had entered its middle phase of dress rehearsal—or would undress rehearsal be more apt? Yes, I suppose so—when my mother poured in. I don't remember why she picked that moment to come home; the joint where she worked had a fire, or she'd made a score for the day, or something. Anyway, she brought a drunken slob of a man with her. All the kids flew out of there as if their own parents had suddenly waltzed in and caught them. I was alone. I was literally caught with my pants down, as we also used to say at the Sorbonne."

Mike noticed that her affect hadn't changed in the least. Whether the experience was factual or a shrewdly conceived fantasy didn't matter. She obviously believed it, and she was recounting it as easily, as painlessly as if it were anything but a recollected trauma.

"The old girl was tanked to the gills," Mrs. Sherwood declared, "but you would've thought I'd swiped that last cup of gin she always needed at bedtime. She yelled at me in front of that slob she'd brought home, and every time I tried to begin to put my clothes on, she'd slap my hand away. She kept screaming oaths about what a bum and a whore I was and I got the feeling after a minute that she wasn't simply putting on a show for her gent friend, but that she was sincerely sore as a boil. She'd never spanked me before, not seriously, but now I had the notion she was going to do it. It may sound funny to you, but for a second I was waiting there for a cuffing around, even hoping for it, if that makes sense."

"Did she?"

"You're not very hip, my friend," she smiled. "That, or you don't understand the reasoning processes of a lush. No, she did not. After she called me every name in the under-thecounter books, she turned to the red-necked sport who was enjoying the spectacle, and ordered him to give me the beating I deserved."

"You say you'd never seen him before."

"That's right, never. Somehow it would've been a little different if I had, if I knew he meant something to the old girl more than a five- or ten-dollar quickie. Well, he went to town. He hesitated for a few minutes and looked at first as though he'd have rather been somewhere else. But there I was, and I guess the weather was nice for it because he began to warm up to the idea. He grinned like a depraved Cheshire cat."

Her curious smile faded briefly. "That miserable son of a bitch beat the living daylights out of me. He started with his hands and then his fists and pretty soon he ripped his belt off and gave me a taste of that. You could've won bets that he'd never had a better time in his life.

"The wild thing was that I yelped, for the most part, only when he cuffed me with his hands, before he really hurt me with those fists and that belt. Once there was pain, I didn't make a sound. When I could, I'd look at her, try to decipher what there was in her, or what had been left out of her, that could let her allow a thing like that to happen. I suppose I've always known more bastards than good people. But there's never been anything that's happened to me since that night to compare with it."

"Did you leave home right away?"

Gradually the smile returned. "The next day. I blacked out and I couldn't move from my cot. I don't mean I fainted or went into hysterics, or anything like that. Call me the gal who's perpetually announcing her engagement to the Marquis de Sade. I spent the night thinking of my mother. Not at all about that man; once he let me go, he didn't enter the picture ever again. I had some absurd idea that in the morning, when we'd be alone and she'd be sober, we could talk, we could reach one another. All right, so I should've dropped my membership in the Pollyanna Corps.

"In the morning," she said, "the old girl was sober, and she even remembered what'd taken place. Do you think she regretted it, do you think she had for a minute the sliver of an understanding of what she'd done? The violence was out of her, but she warned me that if I ever even glanced at a man before it was time to get married, she'd kill me. As simple as that. Period, no exclamation point.

"She went out of the rooming house. I sat on her bed for a while, I don't know how long, maybe a couple of minutes, maybe a half-hour, and then I wondered what I was waiting for. All of a sudden I became the original cucumber. I got up and packed the clothes I wanted. She always kept about fifty or sixty dollars in a special drawer. I took it all and I stuffed as much food from the icebox as I could get into my big. J. C. Penney purse and I hitch-hiked to Dallas.

"In my teens I always looked older, especially when my hair was pulled back in a knot. I got jobs waiting table and the day I was able to do any saving I sent every nickel I'd taken back to the old girl. I worked my way from Texas on to Las Vegas, and finally to Los Angeles. Where I came from, Hollywood and Heaven were considered synonymous."

"You worked your way? Alone, and at fourteen? How?"

Her eyes became slits, but for only a fleck of time. "You can hear what I tell you, Doctor, and then you have the right to report on your pad there that I'm a psychopathic liar, but this is the absolute truth. Nobody would ever ask me to write a treatise on mental health, and I may have a shaky concept of virtue, but never once in my life was I up for auction. I hop in the sack because I'm a friendly sort of person, and for no other reason. I've been there with everyone from Bolivian millionaires to wispy countesses to the letter carrier, but it's always been strictly *pour le sport*. I've been a waitress, a shop girl, a model and an actress, but I want you to know the apple fell far from the tree. I am not my mother's girl."

Symbolically, as if she'd once more overstepped her planned bounds and permitted herself to be caught with her pants down, Mrs. Sherwood sat back, probably astonished by the intensity of feeling she hadn't mean to expose, and became comfortably flip again. Mike attempted to hold her to her pitch of seriousness, however fragile it was, but when she abruptly returned to the safe gagster's ring, he didn't chase after it.

He made furtive shorthand notes as she traced her ascent from one significant bed to another on both Coasts, now and then surprising him with cogent flashes of insight which he wouldn't have expected. When it became abundantly clear that she had shifted gears and was deliberately working to shock him with the robustly lusty details of what unconventional sex practices specifically pleased her, and when she capped the sundae by leisurely disclosing that she currently was having affairs with a man in New York City and with a woman here in Waymouth, he gave up—for this session, anyway.

There was small doubt that Phil Morrow would've given up. In his effectively trained way, Phil would have stood for no nonsense. He would have pursued, like a harsh yet benign taskmaster. He would have directed the subject back to the area which apparently hurt the most and wouldn't have let her slip away. He would have both made her talk it all out and made her see why she needed professional help.

But Mike Crayne was not Phil Morrow. He regarded his notes, hopeful that they would ring helpful bells later in his discussion with Phil. *Superficial, ingenuine quality to relating. Disassociated. Suspicious of validity of subject's overproductiveness. No confidence in what she says. Pretends excessive pride in promiscuity. Feeling tone seldom appropriate to the situation. Good mind, vigilantly intelligent...*

At the conclusion of the session, Mike said, "You've been very helpful, Mrs. Sherwood. May we think of another session, later in the week?"

She brightened perceptibly, and he had the untextured feeling that, under less strained circumstances and free of her compulsive wise-guy defenses, she would have brightened as instinctively and as genuinely if he had told her he would take her to the circus to see the clowns.

"That means I got the part!" she advised, approvingly.

"The part?"

"You and your noblemen don't invite an interviewee back unless her case is particularly interesting. Isn't that so?"

"Did you doubt that you and your 'case' were interesting?"

"That's for one of us to find out, isn't it?" she teased. Still unduly elated, she left the room and closed the door softly behind her.

The remainder of the day's appointments, one tiringly following another with only minor respites, were anticipated carbon copies of subjects he and the others had met in other places.

A plain but pleasant woman. 43. Secretarial college graduate. Three children. Husband in lumber business. Sex twice prior to marriage. First with fiance who was later killed in action in Bougainville. Then with husband, a week before the wedding. Married almost fourteen years, relations with husband essentially satisfactory. No adulteries. Husband could be more romantic before and during act of lovemaking, but no deeply warranted complaints. A good man, solid and sensible, the man she loves and the man next to whom she wants to be buried.

A chubby, pink-cheeked, jolly and craftily uncomplicated woman. 46. High-school education. Five children. Husband a factory foreman. A virgin until marriage. Required what she regarded as a very long time—after the birth of her third child—to relax with sex, but now enjoys it most of the time, and likes husband more, too. Suspects husband committed adultery more than once during early years of marriage, but doesn't mind because she's sure he's not doing it now.

A vapidly pretty, prematurely graying woman. 39. With unimportant differences here and there, a woman with fundamentally the same story as told by the foreman's wife.

A gross, showy, heavy-lipped man. 50. Two diamond rings and a diamond stickpin. Guffaws often and tells a pointlessly filthy joke at the session's outset ("to clear the air"). Two years of high school. Used-car dealer. Married twenty-seven years to dandiest little woman that ever walked this earth. Enormously proud of two children. Fornicates frequently with young call girls, wants to be eminent and popular, feels great self-esteem when he pay as high as $100 to show off a girl at the Latin Quarter. Sees no dichotomy between frequent adulteries and assurance that he is an excellent husband and father. Admits near the end of the session that he has been increasingly impotent for past five years.

On his way back to the hotel, Mike stopped in at a liquor store and bought a fifth of good Scotch. The early evening was open-collar warm and he suspected that Scotch wasn't a warm night's drink, but he felt like drinking and the vodka hadn't done much good.

In the suite, he phoned down for a bucket of ice, showered, donned slacks, and tipped the bellhop a half-dollar for the ice. He built his first drink liberally and, before he took his first sip, regarded his watch. It was exactly three minutes of six. Three minutes of three in California.

What would Valerie be doing now, at three minutes before three? She would be back from her session with her analyst; Farrow never treated private cases after one in the afternoon. She might be "helping out," as she chose to call the unnecessary puttering she did, at her father's dry-goods store. Or she might be home. Valerie had three daily addresses: her father's store, her father's home, and the office of the psychoanalyst her father had purchased for her. She was a grown woman, and there were times when Mike was dizzy with the love of her, but her helpless dependence on her father too often made her at one with the bulk of emotionally arrested women Mike interviewed. He was not against her being in analysis as such. No one knew more acutely than he that she needed the kind of guidance neither a husband nor a parent was equipped to give. What grated at him was that Farrow was not much good, little more than a company spy for her father, a twenty-bucks-a-throw palliative who had encouraged her to remain in five-days-a-week treatment for too many years, and about as dynamic in approach and guidance as a constipated snail.

His subsequent sessions with interviewees after the Sherwood interview today had only served to heighten his inner picture of Mrs. Sherwood, and to make him freshly conscious of the comparisons between her and Valerie. The similarities had nothing to do with Marianne Sherwood as a moral delinquent, a possibly inextricably confused woman who thought she had nothing to give other human beings except her sex organs. Valerie, in most ways, was as chaste in thought and deed as a Carmelite applicant, and often turned a giggling crimson when someone told a mildly off-color story.

The similarities, though, were available for inspection. The capriciousness and the urge to retreat when love promised to be at its most honest. The fear that healthy affection had somehow to be suspect, and the instinctive determination to deal with healthy affection by fighting it off, making fun of it, running way from it. Running to safer quarters. For Marianne Sherwood, it was still the security of the gang bang. For Valerie, it was the prickly but undemanding serenity with her father.

Because he wanted his wife back for good, or out of his life for good, Mike Crayne picked up the receiver, resolutely dialed her California number, and left his drink at the faraway bureau where he'd placed it. It was now or never, by God, and the booze was nothing more than a delaying tactic. He had heard descriptions of delaying tactics and crutches from the first day he'd gone to work for Victor Alders, and every time he had spotted them for what they were.

Valerie lifted her own receiver, and he suspected after the first thirty seconds that she was far from comfortable with him. They talked about the weather in Waymouth and about her father's business and health, and Mike announced that he wanted her to catch the next flight to New York. They could iron out the difficulties once she got here.

"What do you propose I say to Dr. Farrow?" she asked. "Goodbye and good luck? We're working through an extremely vital phase now. I'd think you'd be the last one to recommend canceling treatment."

"I'm recommending that you fly here for a week. One week. A jet can get you here before I say so long and hang up. It's no damn good this way, Val. I love you and I want you here and, Goddammit, you're my wife! You don't belong three thousand miles away from me."

"This isn't the time, Mike," Valerie asserted, and he recognized her familiar, sudden change of tone. She'd always been sharply attuned to the most obscure faltering in his voice. The instant she caught the scent, her own faltering disappeared and she took the reins in her recovered hands. "Dr. Farrow and I are breaking through to new material. My father's not well and business at the store, as I told you, has been worrying him so that—"

"Val," Mike said, standing, his voice hard, "shut up and listen. I've stayed on that flexible string of yours all this time because of my problems, perhaps, not because of yours. We can go into that. Right now I want you to make plans to come here. Your excuses can all go to hell. You're going to arrange for that jet flight, or the divorce you've been dangling in front of me is going to go into the stages of effect immediately. And you can bet your father's bottom dollar I mean that."

Valerie's pause was reminiscent but ominous. When she finally answered him, her usually deliberative voice was too cheerfully matter-of-fact. "Then you do as you see fit, Michael," she rejoined, and Mike sank slowly to the armchair. "I showed good taste in falling in love with you long ago, but my father and Dr. Farrow are right, as usual. You lack patience and understanding, the two things a man in your position ought to have to be a success. And as long as you stay with that Institute of yours, you won't have take-home pay enough to provide for extra pipe tobacco, let alone a wife who's used to the comforts of home."

The words wounded and he frowned. "You've always been complex, Val," he complained quietly and slowly, not in anger any more but in a soddenly dazed, almost admittedly beaten hope to understand this woman he once had believed he understood—big faults, little faults, all faults. "But this is the first time my earning capacity's been a subject for discussion. Are you giving me your philosophy, or your father's and Farrow's?"

"Let's not get into a big thing now, Michael," she said hurriedly, her voice lowering. "Papa just walked in the front door for tea, and there's no need to drag him into any of this. You know how he worries."

"Goodbye, Val."

"Goodbye. Let's talk again sometime."

When the line was clear, and a couple of devastating minutes had passed, Mike Crayne dialed California again. He heard Ben

Robbins' courtroom voice, identified himself, and instructed Ben to go ahead immediately with divorce proceedings.

"Are you sure you want to go through with this, Mike, m'boy?" Ben inquired with his unfettered joviality.

"Are you sure you don't want me to hire another attorney?" Mike snapped. He ordered Ben to write down the Alders itinerary and the hotels where he expected to stay over the next month, and then replaced the receiver.

Anger welled in him. He sought cigarettes and found none. The thought did not occur to him to phone down for a pack. He finished his lightly touched drink in a rude series of swallows and, squinting murderously at the bottle at the far end of the bureau beside the table light, grabbed it by the neck and poured from it until the tumbler was half-filled.

Pacing furiously, he glanced at his watch and conceived of Phil putting in an unannounced appearance. Phil, whose greatest joy while all surrounding buildings were burning to the ground was to rush milk to the Hottentots and to read Aesop to orphans, would detect incipient depression with his built-in radar equipment, and would play an uninvited Uncle Wiggley. Anxious to avoid Phil Morrow who, when all equivocations were said and done, was probably his best friend, Mike hastened through the address book of his mind. Nancy Garrity came to him and he asked the desk operator to buzz her. He was as prepared to pore over Waymouth cases as he was ready to strike a match on a cake of soap.

"I'd much rather have dinner with you, Mike," Nancy confessed, "but I've already promised Nelson. I'm to meet him in the lobby in—let's let me read this watch—in ten minutes."

"That means he's still in his room," said Mike. "Ring him back and beg off. No, don't do that. Whatever you do, don't beg. Tell him Mike Crayne wants to talk with you. Tell him he's been superceded by The Hierarchy. Tell him anything."

"I'll figure something out. Where can I meet you so that he won't be lurking in the bushes?"

"There aren't any bushes for miles around," Mike grumbled. "I'll rap at your door as soon as I'm dressed and we'll go down through the lobby together. We'll get a cab there and find a restaurant."

Mike dressed in his best brown silk suit, scrupulously combed what remained of his hair, and drank some more of the Scotch, although he fully intended to order drinks at the restaurant. Vaguely he remembered that Phil had requested a conference for ten o'clock tonight, a note-matching conference, the quick kind that lasted through the wee hours. Phil, unlike the others, worked straight through with interviews, once the others had gone for the day, and had his meals sent up.

Well, Phil could wait, Mike decided, or he could find professional solace from Nelson. If you worked hard, you once in a while had to cut loose and give relaxation a break.

He collected Nancy at her door and was pleased to see how pretty she was. The elevator dropped them to the lobby where, as each had guaranteed the other, Nelson was hovering. Because Mike was in no mood to make a high production of soothing quivering feelings, and because Nancy automatically sensed his attitude, she released herself from him for a moment to make an unheard peace with Nelson. Returning, she confided, "Nelson's only problem is that he's a little lonely. We're indifferent parents at this point, I guess, but put him in front of a hamburger steak with onions, and he'll be back on the ball within minutes."

In an overheated but recommended Italian restaurant, Mike asked for chianti to follow chianti and they both ordered salad and manicotti, the house's specialty. The dinner and conversation were good, and Mike drank most of the wine. A clown of a waiter hunched at the bar and, as the juke box blared "The Anvil Chorus," punctuated it by crashing the cash register shut at the right moments and singing a decent bass when no punctuation was indicated. The radishes were a blessing. The waiter, whose shabby red jacket had a sewn legend on the wide lapel which tabbed him as Angelo, took a fancy to them and appeared at intervals with obviously rehearsed funny cracks, until Mike discreetly commanded him to butt out.

Nancy wore drop earrings and a gala, beaded purple dress. She was alluringly pretty and she seemed to know that Mike was troubled and that he was drinking continually because he was troubled. Because it was the right thing to do at the time, he told her what had happened. She listened to him, asked intelligent questions when the proper moment came for her to ask them, commented, and summarized in a manner that didn't make him want to haul off and hit her. By the time they returned to the hotel, he mentioned that he had a bottle of Scotch going to waste and why couldn't he bring it to her room?

"Give me five minutes," Nancy said, "and then turn the knob. The door will be unlocked."

Opening her door with his free hand, the hand that didn't hold the bottle, Mike Crayne felt elaborately drunk, but in no mood to wrestle or to talk wrestling. He had hoped, once he closed the door behind him, to find that she had changed into one of those frail negligees, which the slightest touch could wing away. There were slippers on her feet, but otherwise she wore what she had worn in the restaurant. Ah well, he thought, be grateful for small favors. She's not about to noise me out with churchly speeches about her father and her psychoanalyst.

"I forgot the ice," he said, "but I have the idea it's a pool of water by now. We could call Room Service for a bucket."

"Not unless you'd like," she suggested. "A drop or two of faucet water is fine with me."

Mike accepted her two hotel tumblers, poured, and handed her hers. The radio was on, but tuned so low he couldn't make out the song. He settled into the red armchair—her bedroom was identical to his—and, at her invitation, talked out the rest of his marriage. He was poignantly conscious of the strokes and curves of her ripe body. Through gradually filming eyes he regarded the bottle of Scotch at his elbow. The level had gone down, and it occurred to him that he, not she, was doing most of the emptying. He didn't bother to read his watch but assumed after a while that he had talked and drunk far too long, that the minutes had sped by, and that he might have trouble in rising. Her attention was still focused on him, he gathered, and when he lifted himself heavily from the chair at one unidentified point, he made a plunge for her because it seemed to be the right thing to do, because he was blurredly convinced she had given him the sign.

The whiskey he could not handle clouded his head and became his enemy without warning, and he knew the moment he kissed her cheek and mouth and she tolerated him under stiff arms that he had misjudged. He could not back away. Breathing hoarsely, certain in the lone reasoning corner of his brain that he was all the insensitive forms of swine he loathed, he forced himself on her at the bed, and clumsily strove to pin her arms behind her. She struggled, but with no strenuous fight, and he could not understand why she neither greeted him nor shoved him away.

Exhaustion and defeat overwhelmed him within minutes and he rolled away, his breathing still hoarse. "You'd better go," he heard her say, and he recognized he would have to leave her before he could determine whether there was chill or sympathy in her voice. Nodding, he painfully engineered his legs to the floor, hunched forward, and brought himself up.

At her door he reached for the right word to utter. She pulled the door open but would not look at him. He limped to his own door across the hall and, because he could not locate his key, knocked.

Phil let him in. "Hi, sport," Mike acknowledged and weaved to the bathroom, where he was sick. Weakly he undressed as Phil, thank God, didn't hover with windy concern.

He padded to the bed and didn't remember hitting the pillow.

❧ ❧ ❧

Nancy phoned Phil and, pleading a headache, asked to be excused from the ten o'clock conference. Phil inquired if he might stop over for a minute. He had never requested such a thing since she'd known him. Because he surely had seen Mike come in to the suite, and because it was childish to hope he hadn't made some association between her and Mike Crayne's drunkenness (if he couldn't put two and two together, there was always Nelson, dependably standing in the wings with helpful information) she invited Phil to her room.

Hurriedly she smoothed the wrinkles from the bedspread and hid the bottle of whiskey in the closet. She carried the two tumblers and even the crowded ash tray—some cigarettes with traces of dark lipstick, some not—into the bathroom, set them on the floor, and closed the bathroom door. At the bureau mirror she inspected herself. Her face and hair betrayed no fatal secrets, but her tight fitting purple dress had a creased, tampered look, so she changed quickly to a clean, airy, boarding-school blue. By the time she admitted Phil Morrow, she was momentarily reconciled that the room could be vainly rifled by a frothing Gestapo in Search of The Papers.

"Mike's in a pie-eyed coma," Phil disclosed, and Nancy, backing lithely away, was convinced he was examining her critically. "Nelson tells me you and Mike had dinner together."

"That's right," Nancy nodded. "And Nelson probably also told you that Mike came back here with me. But I wasn't the one who put him in his coma, Phil, if that's what you've come to ask."

Phil flared. "Oh, dump that kind of talk! Is that the way you see me—a mother hen out to make her chickens account for themselves? I'm just wondering whether or not I should be worried about him, whether something in particular brought that on or whether he's just plain loaded."

"I'm sorry, Phil. I shouldn't've said that."

"On the other hand," he declared, his voice and eyes softening, "if Mike's all right and he won't bring any big problems to the job tomorrow except a hangover, then the rest of it's none of my business. The meeting can wait."

She weighed the propriety of telling Phil what had been wrong. Conscientiously omitting the faintest inference that Mike had been anything but a gentleman, she told him about Mike's wife.

"The poor slob," Phil said when she finished, "and the funny duck, too. Why couldn't he've told me all along that something was bothering him? Look, Nancy, there's a good chance he'll be too lame tomorrow morning to work his caseload. I realize you're overworked as it is, but I may have to call on you to hold down the fort."

"Of course," Nancy agreed and then added, because she knew that sooner or later she would have to say it, "—ah—Phil, as if you weren't having troubles enough with the hired help, I have a small problem, too."

"I knew it," he grinned. "You want to join a union and strike for shorter hours and higher pay."

"That grin's about to come off your face in a second and a half."

"What's the problem, Nancy?"

Taking a deep breath, she confided, "You said when you put me on the Warner case that Sally Warner would see only a woman. Are there ways to persuade her differently?"

"That's possible," he replied warily. "If you have a reason for not wanting to take her case, I imagine she can simply be advised that you're not available. I think I told you when we were all together in the suite that I'd give a tooth to have the case myself."

Nancy appreciated his making the reneging easier than she would have expected. "I shouldn't admit this to the mandarin, but—well, I'm satisfied that my reason is good, and it's simple, too. The Warner girl likely has a great deal to offer the survey, and I think you're far better equipped to tackle it."

"Who are you to downgrade your own skills?"

"Oh, I'm as skillful as all get-out. I just don't want to go on the sessions with the feeling that someone's around who can handle them better than I can."

"That soft soap won't exactly hurt your future with the Institute, young lady," he kidded. But you'd better keep in mind you're not automatically off the case. We'll jargon it up a little when she arrives, but if she won't hold still to be interviewed by a man, I'll expect you to be prepared with your operating gloves. A fresh rape doesn't present itself to us every day in the week. This one's too good to let go."

" 'Fresh rape.' You're getting more clinical and less humane in your old age, Doctor Morrow."

"Don't quibble over my phraseology. You just got through saying I have the most brilliant mind of the Twentieth Century."

"So I did. I'll be available, Phil. And thanks."

Phil started for the door, but paused to turn as he thought of something. Both the early anger and the later teasing were missing, and in their place was the thoughtful smile of a good friend.

"I hope Mike didn't say anything to offend or upset, Nancy."

"Why—would you think that?"

"Because I'm still the brilliant man and I know you pretty well. You're a sensitive person with an unconfessed belief that a guy who goes on even an occasional bender ought to stay in the case histories, where he belongs. I have no idea of what Mike said, or how he said it, beyond what you told me. But if he got bitter and talked out of turn, chalk it up to the fact that he's not the sophisticated boozer he thinks he is, and laugh it off. He not only knows his job inside out, he's also the nicest fella that ever lived."

Afraid to hear more interpretations of herself, interpretations she knew were false, Nancy thanked him again and saw him out. Undressing, she lighted a cigarette and thought, How could a man as knowledgeable as Phil be so wrong? Mike Crayne was very drunk and tried as hard as he was physically able to make love to me, Dr. Morrow. I was the refined girl from Minneapolis while he fumbled, but the last thing in the world I would've done would be to stop him. You don't know that, sensitive Dr. Morrow.

And there is the horrible fear that when Mike wakens, filled with remorse, he won't know it, either.

But, all of a marvelous sudden, I do.

At dinner in the extravagant East Side restaurant he was unwaveringly attentive. He ordered special foreign dishes she had never heard of, much less tasted, and he listened to her every word as if he couldn't be more interested. He told her, without sounding like an old lecher, that at the store he was Mr. Sherwood, but that here his name was Steve.

They sat in fourth-row-center seats at the theatre, and the show—the fifth she had ever seen on Broadway—was fun. Threading up the aisle when it was over, Steve gently squeezed her arm and asked if she'd like to have some supper. "It's up to you," Sally said. They rode in a taxi to the parking lot, claimed his Fiat, drove in embarrassed semisilence until they were out of the tangled Manhattan traffic, and checked into a motel on the highway somewhere between New York and Waymouth.

The room and all the effects in the room were so impersonal that when he bolted the door after him and turned to smile at her, suddenly small beside the bed, the word *adultery* had all but disappeared.

"You're frightened," he said, sidling toward her.

"Just a little bit."

"There's no reason to be."

"I know," she answered, and managed a smile just a fleck of a moment before he touched her. She asked him to switch off the overhead light. Steve did, but the white blinds at the windows seemed to pour in even more light. The sound of cars purring past was an intrusion. She needed more minutes than she would have thought to become inured to the sounds.

In the dark they undressed, almost solemnly. As his warm hand traced over her bare shoulder and as she responded with a night love which segued from ecstacy to emptiness, there was the overriding feeling of being lost, being homesick. But the feeling was not the one she had had with Guv Barnes. This man, Steven Sherwood, was, for all the seedy, transient atmosphere, the first grown-up man who'd ever wanted to love her. She had told him about Bob, about the park. She had detailed the awfulness. There had been any number of opportunities for him to play on the awfulness. He hadn't. He belonged to another woman, she knew, and their being here in this homeless place was wrong, but she had never known anyone so considerate and kind.

They stayed in the motel for only minutes longer than an hour. They kissed, made a perhaps understandably hasty love, dressed, smiled at each other, walked out to the Fiat, and slid in. On the painfully long ride to Waymouth, Sally laced her fingers over her knees and recalled they hadn't shared more than a dozen words with one another throughout their hour.

"Good night," said Steve tenderly, yards away from the door. "I'll see you again soon, I hope."

"When?"

"Soon. Very soon. Suppose you take off tomorrow and rest up. I'll give you a buzz. Don't worry about anything."

"I—think I love you, Steve," Sally exclaimed, and thought she saw him stiffen.

"Good night, dear." He touched her knee and brushed his lips past her forehead, but he said nothing else.

In her house, with the door closed, emptiness enveloped her.

⚜ ⚜ ⚜

When Marianne returned home, in imperative need of a drink, Mrs. Quigley told her a Mr. Gibbs had phoned and would wait for her to phone back. She fixed a stiff gin and tonic, light on the tonic, and took it out to the patio. For some idiotic reason she no longer could remember, Mr. Gibbs was the name she'd advised Dan Parrish to use when he telephoned her.

Sinking into one of the deck chairs, her entire body ached and she realized how exhausting the interview had been. The interview *and* the series of belly punches from Aaron Miles' office and Dan. She had never admitted to anyone as much as she had admitted, within the period of an hour, to that psychologist. There had been the numberless times, when she had trusted a particular person, or when she'd wished to shock just for the pure enjoyable hell of it, that she had confided bits and pieces of her past, censoring as she chose. But today had been different. Today she had opened most of the long-stuck portholes, simply because nothing about that attractive young man named Crayne implied he was going to gobble her up.

What, Marianne thought without emotional fury as she gazed out over the lawn, is to become of me? As they used to squeal in those self-consciously naughty plays about the deep Say-outh, how can I breathe?

The props had been kicked from under her, and for fair. To Dan Parrish, who represented the constant registrar of her constant youth and desirability, she was a fading old bag—or whatever it was he'd whispered to that curly-locked, firm-knockered teen-ager at the telephone.

To Aaron Miles' girl lieutenant—and why don't we face up to it, kids, and then merrily pitch the goblets into the fireplace? to Aaron Miles himself—she was a strident exactress. And who in his right mind wants to invite a strident ex-actress, especially one who'd never been very talented, anyway, up to the house for barbecues? The Manhattan and Hollywood hills are overpopulated with curly-locked, firm-knockered girls, just gratefully released from confining puberty, who can out-act Eleonora Duse and romantically accommodate picture executives simultaneously.

To her husband Steve, former *Boy's Life* subscriber, who wanted the sort of wife who could brighten the country-club halls merely by entering and quoting her husband's latest joke, she was a drunken bust, a melancholy failure. Over and over again he had come to her, anxious to reach her, to know her. Over and over again the meaningless restlessness had scooted her away. Their marriage had promised to be sound, long ago when he'd brought her to Waymouth, and she'd been determined to forget her stalled career and the fun life. To his credit, Steve had stuck by her over those first serious bumpy roads. What are you supposed to do, though? Wear a sandwich board which reads *Neurotic Dame, Keep Your Distance?*

To her liquor, she was slowly but surely becoming an object that could be manipulated without half a struggle. Sober, or in the better days when liquor still was her buddy, she might have gone to Julia Havilland's home for a few games. But as a tortured beggar? Hardly. That was the hard sauce's doing.

The smart thing to do, of course, would be to pull up stakes, pack, and vamoose. The question was, to where? And how, on no savings, no significant cash other than the measly private account of possibly $1,000 at Enright Trust? With $1,000 you could get, with monumental luck, as far away as the corner grocery.

Steve was worth a sizable amount, as he'd once derived a boot out of informing her before he'd stopped informing her of anything, but the vital purse strings were held by his father. The ancient duddy's concept of marriage was one in which the wife rolled over and salivated in worship every time her husband came within a mile of her. If the marriage didn't work out, that was too bad but doubtless it was the wife's fault. If there were no children after a year or so, the fault lay incontestably with the wife (She: "You know what a gruesome mother I'd make, Steve. I know me. I'd swell all those months in those treacherous maternity clothes and everyone would gawk at me on the street as though I'd just left the zoo. There's nothing in me, in my makeup, to guarantee I'd take proper care of a child." He: "Nobody's demanding guarantees, Marianne. Let's try." She: "No. It's an impossible thing to even suggest.").

If she were to take a walk, and to be wholly dependent on her own resources, she would be flat broke inside of a month. The thought of punching a time clock, actually or symbolically, made her want to gag.

If she waited, though, she would be a Sherwood widow. The image of herself walking down the dusty road in black caused her to shudder, but then black was what widows were supposed to wear, wasn't it?

As a Sherwood widow, she was entitled to what still could pass for a fortune. She had followed the lineage. The previous Sherwood widows who had behaved themselves estimably, Rachael Sherwood, Ida Sherwood, Frederika Sherwood and Laura Sherwood, had lived out their lives in ideal, thigh-deep fiscal comfort. Take good care of your Sherwood husband, the rule went, and the largesse will drop from the heavens.

If you weren't a Sherwood widow, however, and if the geezer in charge of the checkbook didn't fawn kindly on you if you elected to take a powder, the order was ineluctable. You couldn't collect as much as a subway token. You were sent on your way....

Marianne ambled back to the living room from the patio for a refill and thought of Dan's call. The doubts were so few that she could lay a heavy bet. She was a dreary old bag, but she wasn't; you could read tomorrow morning's *Herald Tribune* and inspect the official denials. Dan didn't want to lose her as a playmate. She was getting old, and no comparison to the girl children with the curly locks and high, small bosoms, but the cold winter was on its inexorable way and you never could judge when you might need a trusty old bag to warm your feet.

Dan answered on the first ring.

"Hello, Mr. Gibbs," she greeted.

"Can you talk?"

"Oh, boy, can I talk!"

"About that call—"

"The lady who picked up your phone was a niece in from Cleveland. She was showing you the family album and she was just up to the 1919 begats when I so rudely interrupted."

"It's not quite that gluey, but almost. The answer will kill you. Baby, get in the car and come here. I'll have your favorite soda pop on tap, and I'll explain everything in detail." Marianne, silent, made him wait, made him sweat "Baby?"

"Who was the chick, Dan?"

"You come here and the grog will be in abundance."

"The grog. Does that tell my story, beginning to end? If the grog is in abundance, I can be wound like a watch?"

"Methinks thou doth protest too—"

"I'm ready to leave these suburban surroundings you find so funny, Dan, and move to the city to marry you. Getting divorced is no issue. If I meet you without a wedding band, will you be at home to me?"

"Baby .. ".

"Will you spend two weeks with me? Fourteen whole nights in a row? I'm asking as straight as can be, Dan."

"Let's—ah—have a drink on it, right?"

"Would you like to have me with you for longer than three or four hours at a single time, Dan? Would you—tell me here and now—would you like for me to pack up my old kit bag and move in there with you?"

"You're fried, baby."

"I happen to be sober, baby. Thank you for your definitive answer. Don't take any wooden nickels, baby."

Marianne replaced the receiver and the knitted thought of being a Sherwood widow, now dreadful, now realistic, flushed through her. Steve, for all his inadequacies, was not a mustache-twirling villain. But the sole thing which kept her from good money and kept her continually asking for the brand of odious vulgarity the Dan Parrishes fed her was Steve. If he were out of the way, if she could suavely push him out of a speeding plane, there would never again be the damnable threat of poverty. She could tell all the Dan Parrishes, as she had told this Dan Parrish, to turn a royal blue.

Bringing her refill back to the patio—the only part of the vile house in which she could feel unconditionally free—she wondered what it would be like to murder Steve. One of her mother's real or imagined husbands—Sammy Boal, the bulky, coarse-haired, six-footer with the honest-to-God knife scar slashed across his cheek—had committed a murder. There had been some kind of argument during a crap game and Sammy had risen to choke a man to death. The police pounced, but he hadn't even gone to trial.

The remembrances from the conveniently stashed corners of the past were goofy and uncalled for, certainly, but then why had that snoopy Dr. Crayne inveigled her to open all the airless doors?

Without announcement, the thought of murder intrigued Marianne and she walked back to the living-room phone. She dialed Julia Havilland's number. A man answered. "May I speak with Mrs. Havilland?" she inquired.

Julia was on the line in seconds. "Mrs. Sherwood? It's so nice to hear from you."

"You have a hundred and eighty extension phones in your house. I have, too."

"No."

"That's pleasant to hear. Julia, my hubby is slaving away at the office. Could I talk you into dropping over for five-point and—ah—whatever it is girls are expected to do with five-point?"

"I was waiting for you to call."

"I'm calling."

"Thirty minutes?"

"Good enough. I'll be waiting."

Julia's voice got a little louder, a little jollier. "A card game sounds fine, Marianne. If my husband doesn't have any objections, I can be there in half an hour."

Satisfied with herself, Marianne strode back to the bar. If you wanted to leave the room, you could wring your hands and smack the inkwell to the floor. But it was always simpler to merely raise your hand and have the teacher recognize you.

CHAPTER FIVE

❧ ❧ ❧

"Y OU'D NEVER seen this Polumbo boy before that night in the park?" Phil asked.

"No, only that one time," said Sally Warner.

"You've discussed your fiance, and your father, and Guv Barnes, and Steven Sherwood, but you haven't talked about Vincente Polumbo."

"I—just don't think about him."

"Not at all?"

The Warner girl was remarkably pretty and brighter than he had been led to anticipate, but Phil was curiously surprised that she talked as freely as she did. She had had to be persuaded to accept a male interviewer, and there had been a natural awkwardness at the beginning of the hour, an understandable reluctance to touch all bases. But once she got going, she talked as if the barrel had no bottom. He had interviewed scores of subjects before who leapt too quickly and too agreeably into the fire, anxious to tell far more than was requested.

That wasn't exactly true of Sally Warner. She stayed within the bounds of appropriate confidence. It was entirely possible that she spoke as freely as she did, Phil decided, for the cloudless reason that until now she'd had one, who cared, to talk to.

"I thought about him a lot afterwards, in the hospital," she answered. "I couldn't tell anyone, not even Dr. Maslyn, but I hated him more than anyone or anything I'd ever hated in my life. My father was making a lot of talk about getting friends together from his private club he belongs to, and going after him with guns and a rope. I knew that's what my father thought everybody expected him to say, so he said it; he's always threatening to get his friends to do some kind of brave thing with him, but that's all he's ever done: threaten. He doesn't even have any real friends. They drink with him at this club and they kid him, but I doubt if he knows more than two people who'd go out of their ways to do anything at all for him.

"I've never been vengeful, toward anyone. But I hated that boy for taking so much from me—my boy friend and...for attacking me." She paused. "For a while I honestly wanted my father to do what he said he was going to do. I wanted that boy caught, punished. I'd come out of sleep, and I'd think about him being dead, the way he'd made Bob dead, and I wanted that."

"You say 'for a while' you wanted it. Why just for a while?"

"Because I found out about him. He was—I think the word Doctor Maslyn used was 'deranged.' He was as responsible for everything as the man in the moon. There was no way to blame him, to blame anybody. Father Chalmers came to see me at the hospital; he runs this home where the boy stayed. He wanted to take some of the responsibility if it would make me feel better, because he imagined he should've suspected the Polumbo boy was that disturbed. That was ridiculous, of course. Blame...Bob's mother was sure she knew where to place the blame. On me. Not on the Polumbo boy. On me. Maybe that's ridiculous, too, maybe it isn't."

"Certainly it is," Phil said softly, supportively.

"I asked to see Mrs. Raymond. To talk with her. But I guess it's just as well she wouldn't see me; I wouldn't've known what to say to her."

"Did you love Bob?"

"We were going to be married."

"Yes, I know that. But did you love him?" Phil repeated and then added, "That might well be much too complicated a question to answer with a yes or no."

She appeared to be embarrassed that she didn't reply at once. "You're right; it is a complicated question. Isn't it funny? No one except Bob ever asked me that. No one except Bob really asked me much of anything.

"If I had to give an answer fast, though, one way or another, I think I'd have to say no," she went on slowly, inspecting her hands. "I know it's a shameful thing to admit, isn't it? What I told myself when I agreed to marry him was that he was a good man, and that I'd do everything I could to be a good wife. I'm sure I would've come to love him. He was an awfully quiet boy—never had much to talk about, and I suppose if I'd had my choice I would've picked a different type of boy—but I would've been as good a wife as possible."

"If you'd had your choice? You're twenty-one years old, intelligent, and extremely pretty. I would think you'd have scads of young men running after you."

She smiled tolerantly. "This is Waymouth, New York. Everyone claims we're close to the most cosmopolitan city in the world, but none of it ever rubbed off onto us. We used to think the people who moved here from the city after the War would change things a little, but nothing's changed. The Underwood people mingle and marry with the Underwood people. The working people mingle and marry with the working people.

"I've lived on Griswold Street from the day I was born. That's factory neighborhood. Nobody's really poor there, but it's still a shabby part of town, and nobody cares much about brightening it up. My father is a night watchman, and one who drinks a lot and gets mean, at that. He's sort of the town joke to people, if they don't despise him. He's still fighting his grandfather's war. I said before that for a while I hated Vincente Polumbo, but if I think of hate the way my father thinks of hate, then I'm using the wrong word. He tried to teach my sister to hate and to teach me to hate, but we weren't as good at it as he is.

"He's always hated, because he's a failure in just about everything, and that hatred must help him. He hates me because my mother died delivering me; that happened twenty-one years ago, but when he's extra drunk and extra mean he still tells me he'd have his wife if it hadn't been for me. He hates Catholics and colored people and Jews and Spanish people and—oh, you know, all people. My sister Frances is eleven years older than I am. She's as decent a person as ever lived, and she'd make any man the best wife you could imagine, but she'll never get married. He couldn't teach her to hate, but he was able to teach her to be scared—first of him and then of everything. The poor thing, sometimes it's as though I were older and she were the kid sister. I try to talk sense to her, tell her to get out, move into Manhattan, move out to another state, away from him. You'd think I was telling her to set fire to him or something. She knows his faults, probably even better than I do, but she stays."

"So do you."

"What?"

"You're an adult. Why don't you take your own apartment, or do as you advise your sister to do: move out of Waymouth?"

She looked away and nodded. "I know that," she said in little more than a whisper. "Bob would still be alive if I'd been strong and left that terrible house. But I'm not strong. My father was good once. Maybe it sounds crazy, but I guess I've been waiting for him to be good again."

Phil waited and said nothing.

"We were talking about Bob," she said. "I couldn't quite see where I was headed. The Waymouth boys I would've liked to date didn't ask me out. The ones who did ask me, the ones who didn't mind my father, were the ones he'd hop on right away. He said that when I got married, it would have to be to someone very special, a professional man. The trouble was, there weren't any professional men interested in Will Warner's daughter.

"Then Bob Raymond came along. He wasn't what my father meant by a professional man, but he was a school teacher, and you could say he had a certain standing in town. His mother was dead set against Dad, but he somehow passed most of Dad's tests and—I don't know—to be frank, without saying anything against Bob, I didn't think any other white knights were going to come storming up to the castle on Griswold Street."

She looked up sharply. "That sounds like I'm whining, doesn't it? Yes, I can hear it and it does. I don't mean it to sound that way—not entirely, anyway." She allowed herself a shy grin. "What I'm getting at is—well," she declared rather than inquired, meeting his eyes, "what is it I'm getting at? I seem to just talk."

"You're not used to talking, are you? Talking out, I mean, to people who won't set themselves up as critics."

"You're right," she nodded, agreeing hesitantly. "But I can't go searching for scapegoats forever, the way my father does. Most of my problems were made by me. I know that."

"How do you know that?" Phil prodded.

"I told you about the boy from high school; Guv Barnes. I told you about Steven Sherwood. I brought them on myself; neither of them twisted my arm. I went into detail about the insane way I behaved when Guv Barnes phoned me and almost announced out loud what he wanted; any other time I wouldn't've even looked at him. I told you about being so —available to Steven. No one forced me. How long can I go on blaming others for the crazy things I do?"

"Do you intend to see Sherwood again?" Phil asked, and he saw her instinctively bite her lip.

"Yes, I think so. If he wants me to."

"Is he there for you?"

"What do you mean?"

"Make believe for a moment that he's not married, that there are better things ahead than single hours spent in motels. Is he honestly the best man you could find? If you were suddenly to need him—for any of a dozen purposes important to you, to no one else living but Sally Warner—would he be there for you?"

"You don't want me to see him again."

"Want? I'm not your analyst, Miss Warner," Phil said gently. "I think all I'm doing is asking you questions you've been asking yourself. What does it matter what *I* want?"

"He's a good man. He listened to me and he was considerate of me. I repeat. He didn't tie my arms and legs and force me into that motel."

"Then let me ask it another way. You said there was a difference between Guv Barnes and Sherwood. You accepted Barnes as a sexual object at the outset, and consciously on no other basis. You imply you would've gone the whole way with him in his car that night if he hadn't been so recklessly insensitive. You went to the motel with Sherwood after how many hours with him away from the department store? Six? Eight? And you'll see him again because, you also imply, he's sensitive to you and the opposite of Barnes. What I asked you was, do you believe at this point that Sherwood would be there for you for anything other than sex?"

"And if I'm interested myself only in sex?"

Sitting back, Phil hoped he had hidden the wince. "You'll excuse me, Miss Warner, but horse feathers. That's foolish talk, and you're not a fool. You are in the market for ego, not for speedy trips to motels."

The blunt declaration, he could tell, got home to her. She faced him, with more serious inquiry than before.

The hour was up. He wanted to keep going, but others were waiting. "Will you come again the day after tomorrow?" he asked.

"I'm—afraid to take off any more time from work."

"Then we'll arrange it after you leave your job. If you call back here later today, there'll be an evening appointment set up."

Rising, she stood carefully away from him.

"I'll call. Thank you."

"Thank *you*, Miss Warner."

Before the next interviewee was shown into the room, Phil glanced over his sparse notes on Sally Warner. *Lacks ego, exposes self to unsavory relationships... Traumatic frigidity based on shock, compensates by charade of mild nymphomania... No needs pro help as much as she thinks.*

The notes would suffice for consultation and later annotation, but, Phil spotted, they actually added up to next to nothing. Sally Warner's problems were large, but she was far less crippled, far more able to handle her problems than a galaxy of overfed women he had interviewed with infinitely fewer troubles.

For a fleck of time he fantasied himself with her on a date. He had had fantasies in the past about subjects he had interviewed, but he'd made himself rudely awaken instantly. Such fancies were out of the question.

Since his trip to Marston City, though, and the flight to Waymouth, dat ole debbil had once again arisen. The urge to drop what he was doing for the Institute for a period of time and find a girl. The all-work-and-no-play syndrome from which he was again finding it hard to release himself on cue. A long time ago Dr. Alders had sat with him in one of those abnormally transient hotel rooms and, transparently testing him, had asked him what his feelings were when the unusually tasty-looking women inferred that they could be had, secrecy guaranteed, after office hours. There inevitably were giftbearing women within a series of interviews.

"I gaze longingly with my third eye," he'd confessed, "and occasionally wish the law of the jungle prevailed. But it never does in surveys, so I merely watch my step."

"You might as well know it," Dr. Alders had confided. "That jungle law possibility has always been a thorn in my side in these surveys. To the bulk of subjects, we're faceless interviewers. We're no power wielders. But to a small per cent we represent that great phallus from on high. I've never told this to anyone, Phil, but I had to let a predecessor of yours go. He was fantastically good and when I fired him I had the image of sawing off both my arms. You know the man I mean."

"Foley."

"Right, and I'll thank you to keep your trap shut. Foley was outstanding, but he came across one too many of the Jollies. He interviewed a divorcee in—let me think now—Davenport. She'd kept so much of her story to herself for so long, evidently, that when he questioned her, the floodgates opened. As I understand it, she invited him to a home-cooked dinner because he looked scrawny from too many restaurant meals. He nobly refused, reciting the Alders Institute pledge, but later he had second thoughts and her telephone number. Oh, you can figure the rest. It was autumn, and his sap was running high, and he went there, and the news got back to me."

"How high did the sap run? Maybe he was hungry for a home-cooked dinner."

Alders' voice had not changed but there was no doubt he had been livid. "That doesn't strike me as much of a mature response, Morrow. The Army would've referred to it, perhaps, as fraternization. The widow lady was no enemy, but I choose to call what Foley did fraternization, too. His place, in terms of our survey, was nowhere but at his desk. What in the hell does it matter whether he slept with her or ate her fried chicken?"

"You're right," Phil conceded.

"We're on trial, every step of the way. The acceptance of our mission came long and hard, and we're getting cooperation now, for the most part, in all cities and towns of the United States. But vigilance remains the watchword. We're all human, but the minute one of us gets out of line, for even an instant, we're in danger of kissing the meat of the project goodbye. I may be overly cautious, but I believe that."

And certainly Dr. Alders was right. You were on the team because you believed in the survey. When your libido raised a fuss, you were on your own but it was vital to deal with it with impeccable manners.

Phil Morrow would never provide an arena for anguish. He was the youngest of five sons in a family of mill workers in Wheeling, West Virginia. Danny, Art, Tim and Spencer had elected to join Pop in the mill. Phil had said he wanted to go to school. The others had gawked at him, as if he'd exclaimed he wished to bomb the Capitol. Pop had taken him aside and advised him that the breeze was heavy out there, but Mom had grasped him and advised that if school was what he desired, school was what he'd get. He strove, and got a scholarship to Carnegie Tech. He broke his engagement to Anna Mae Kasaltski, who lived on Wheeling's border, wept with her for surely an hour, and clumped guiltily to Pittsburgh. He majored in psychology there, played a middling clarinet in a downtown cafe, learned on Saturdays how to butcher cows, and wended his way cordially through a brace of affairs with girls from the drama department.

He got engaged twice, once to a dopey redhead named Agnes Alger, whose only two claims to fame were that she had a season pass to the Pittsburgh Playhouse Lounge because of her parents' subscription and that she had written the lengthiest thesis ever on Pavlov, and next to a superabundant actress named Darlene Weinberg who was remarkable in *Lady Windermere's Fan, The Circle,* and in the hay.

Both engagements were broken in time.

His B.A. from Carnegie Tech led to an M.A., which led to a Ph.D. Dr. Alders found him and took him on.

He had done his very best. The moral of Chip Foley was not lost. Sally Warner and all the Sally Warners were highly possible game. But if you were going to do your job, an important job, you passed up the delicious desserts and you let well enough alone. You were as careful as could be.

Phil finished his interviews and returned to the hotel, where the conference awaited him. Sitting at the head of the imaginary table, he knew he could block out all the Sally Warner thoughts.

In the suite's bedroom, the group listened to Mike's report on Marianne Sherwood and agreed unanimously that her productions were not coherent enough to benefit the survey or, because time was so limited, herself.

"I said I'd see her again," Mike admitted, "which might have been a mistake. I thought at the time that with one or two more sessions with her I could coax her into going for private help, but I've given it some second thoughts and you seem to be backing up those second thoughts. She's disturbed, but she's much too defensive to be coaxed into anything outside of an afternoon roll on the lawn" (*he wanted to hurtle through the nearest window the instant he used the phrase, and he kept his eyes steadfastly averted from Nancy, who sat uneasily to his right*). "Certainly two or three more meetings with her wouldn't persuade her she needs treatment."

"That makes sense," Nelson maintained. "She can be phoned and told her information in the first interview was sufficient."

Phil wrangled briefly about her. He mentioned, in passing, that her husband had had or still was having an affair with one of his subjects, the Warner girl, and that fact alone perhaps recommended further sessions. The others reminded him that the list of volunteers had grown since their first day here and that it was important to meet as much of a cross-section as possible. They discreetly but firmly outvoted him. Phil argued his point for another minute, but conceded they likely were right.

Nelson discussed his caseload up till now, in an earnest, rapid voice, and concluded that he had already probably reached a norm which the upcoming days of interviews would merely bear out. So far he had met eighty per cent adult women, fifteen per cent adult men, and five per cent teen-agers. If the information he'd received was completely accurate—and he was suspicious of the truth of only three or four subjects—there were more instances of current, sustained adultery here, proportionately, than in the last half-dozen cities they had visited. Only a handful of men committed adultery, and then in Manhattan. No Waymouth man he had yet met was having a sideline romance in or immediately near Waymouth. The men, by and large, worked long, exhausting hours to provide elegantly for their wives and some were distinct coronary candidates. The women, by and large, were surfeited with materialism but were unswervingly convinced they were right in demanding more from their husbands, more of everything. The more possessions they obtained, the more they believed they had carte blanche to cuckold their husbands. All their neighbors were sleeping with men who weren't their mates, so that made it socially acceptable. Very few of them confessed to suffering the vaguest pangs of guilt.

Nelson found that most Waymouth teen-age girls were either non-virgins or soon would be. Again proportionately, they were more unhealthily obsessed with sex than the teenage girls in the last half-dozen cities. They had learned from their mothers, doubtless through osmosis, that intercourse with husbands was seen in terms of reward or punishment; many of the girls believed that it would be usual, if not precisely normal, to give themselves to husbands if they received gifts, and to deny husbands if they didn't. Most of the Waymouth teen-age boys, on the other hand, were primarily interested in education and sports, in upstanding competition.

Nelson found no homosexuality among the Waymouth adult men. He did, however, find a considerable amount of it among Waymouth adult women. Only a scattering of them appeared to have any shame over what they were doing, or what they had done.

Nancy saw no evidences of homosexuality among the people she had so far interviewed in Waymouth, except for a scant few cases—all in the past—among a minority of teenagers. Unless the quality of her caseload shifted radically in the oncoming days, there was no more adultery in Waymouth than elsewhere, proportionately or otherwise. She agreed with Nelson that there seemed to be a marked involvement here with owning as much as or more than the Joneses, and that here and there the involvement was related to the bestowal or denial of intercourse, but her findings had not been nearly so devastating as his. She did observe a sizeable amount of admitted sexual unrest, but she couldn't yet define a discernible trend. "I'd like to pass on it until I can study the final computation," she said. "I'm sure there's a specific correlation between the unrest and the very fact of surburbia, but let's wait till all the ballots are in."

Listening to her, a fresh wave of remorse closed in on Mike. He had wakened with the queasy feeling that his legs and arms were chained to the bed, that an army of horses in fur boots had marched throughout the night over his tongue. Phil had extended instantaneous sympathy and had offered him part of the day off. He had shakily answered that he'd do his damnedest to rise from his death bed and go to work. He had groaned and cursed mournfully for several minutes and then suddenly remembered the finale in Nancy's room. He had called upon the Lord to be benign and strike him dead.

After a healing bath and an unsteady cup of black coffee, he had phoned her and asked her to kindly not send for the paddy wagon. To his surprise, she had been perfectly civil to him, and went so far as to share in mourning his hangover. She hardly broadcast it, but he had the weird idea, once he replaced the receiver, that she was sorry only because he'd been unable to complete what he'd set out to do. Now, pinchedly regarding her from only the corner of his eye, he thought about seeing her again.

When the conference ended and Nancy and Nelson left the suite, Phil indicated his concern about Nelson. "I might be completely off-base, but I don't think so. Is there any chance that he's stacking the deck?"

"Anti-wives and pro-hubbies?" Mike asked and Phil nodded. "Why would he do that?"

"That's what I want to know, if it's true," Phil said.

"I'd tend to doubt it, sport. Of course there's no true objectivity in anything and we bring at least a drop of our own shadings into every statistic, but Nelson's good at what he does. He has his quirks, sure, but he wouldn't go out of his way to rig his information. Maybe he's found what he says he's found. Maybe the town's crawling with dykes and broads working their men to death."

"I haven't found an excess of it You haven't. Nancy hasn't."

"Are you worried about the kid?"

"Not yet, but I assure you my eye stays on him until something proves I shouldn't. There's no place in our work for a guy who's flirting with the deep end."

"Speaking of the deep end, boss," said Mike, "I appear to have gone off it last night. The word 'cockeyed' never rammed home to me as fluently as it did last night Or should I say fluidly?"

"So what? I'm making an appointment to get good and sozzled myself one of these nights. I'll expect you to be around to help navigate me."

Mike wondered whether he should say it, and then said it. "My wife and I are getting a divorce, Phil."

"Oh?"

"Very non-committally spoken," Mike grinned. "You're a crummy actor, pal. I can see you know all about it. Either Nancy told you or I told you during my liquid state."

"Nancy told me. I went to see her after you folded up. I just wanted to make sure you were all right. As for her spilling the beans—"

"Hell, I don't mind."

"—she didn't want to say anything, but I made her. Once I found out, I was sorry I'd butted in on something that didn't concern me."

"Did she—also inform you of the wondrously gentlemanly way I behaved in her room?" Mike questioned, tightening, hoping that what he'd done was a locked secret between Nancy and him.

"No. I wasn't there that long. And will you please stop wringing your hands because you got loaded? My God, you'd think you'd written on the wall of a Christian Science church."

Because Phil was interested as a friend, Mike told him about Valerie, about the bumpy marriage and about the end of it. As he talked he discovered that some of the loss's pain already had dissolved.

At dinner, Nancy was animated and gay. The sodden self-pity was out of Mike and he had the happy impression he was in pretty good form, too. She was livelier and less tense than he had ever seen her. They took a bus to a movie and ate popcorn and licorice in the balcony. They walked the mile back to the hotel, talking about everything but the survey and the gymnastics of the night before. At her door, she gave no sign that she wanted to invite him in, and he scrupulously stayed clear of pressing it. He kissed her, lightly and without the hint of implication, and she responded in the same way.

They saw each other over the next days and evenings, whenever they were free. They laughed often and seemed to talk incessantly. They steered clear of all subjects prickly and obviously personal, not because they had vocally agreed to, but because each sensed the time was not right yet, that they would know when it was.

Then there came the middle of an afternoon when, having decided to rearrange their appointment schedules, they also decided to take a drive. Mike rented an open-top roadster and they drove away from Waymouth, past Suffern and Monroe, and up the lazy sideroads which led to the Catskills. Nancy held an upstate map on her lap and snapped merrily that he had a lousy sense of direction and he was going all wrong, but, because they were headed nowhere in particular, it didn't matter.

The day was comfortably warm and, when they spotted a public swimming pool, they parked, rented bathing suits, and raced one another in the water like the happiest of irresponsible children. They had wine and dinner at a small candlelight restaurant, where the mood changed from one of subdued giddiness to one of increasing intimacy. On the ride back toward Waymouth, they were silent for long stretches of time. Then they looked across the road and saw, lighted up in the evening, a big, splendid motel. There was no cheapness to the motel, no suggestion of transience.

"Mike," Nancy said. Her voice was strained but he knew she was sure of herself. "Would you take me there and make love to me?"

In his arms she was frightened, so intensely frightened that the thought struck Mike that he possibly was her first man. When the light was off and she once more asked him to make love to her, he discovered that he was. He held her and he was patient. He asked her if she wanted to talk and she replied in a murmur, "Not now. Later, yes, lots of talk, but not now, dearest."

He was lovingly tender as he helped her and taught her, and she spoke only once again, to tell him she was grateful for his patience. The sounds of voluptuous and at the same time seraphic music wafted in from another room, perhaps another floor, and he was pleased that if there had to be even the minutest interruption that it was this kind of music.

Despite the darkness he could see her, and he saw more than the comely, momentarily bewildered face, the beautiful breasts and the outstretched naked arms. He saw the infinite goodness, and the wonder was that he had seen her for so many months and hadn't seen that.

Presently she was ready for him and she met him in unmistakable love. She called out to him in terror and pain and bliss, and then there was silken peace.

In the speeding days that followed the interview with Dr. Partridge, there was little time for feelings of guilt. Julia saw Marianne at every possible opportunity and was delighted that Marianne was just as eager to see her.

There was no question that Marianne had changed. The blunt language, designed to shock, was missing now, and in its place was sweetness, gracious consideration.

Because there were duties to be performed at home, chores to do for Charles, Julia did them, but now there was only rarely an unglued tenor to her existence. She could even see Charles more clearly now, more compassionately, see him as an eternally good man who wished nothing more in life than to be a good man, blind to the magic of specific arousal, intent on propounding all charity that began away from home.

At intervals during the first week after he'd come back from Spokane, she would regard him in the guaranteed places about the house she had witnessed him in before. In his favorite ever so deep slightly, armchair, the floor checking lamp beaming receipts, licking cordial his nuances lips over his large head. On the flowered couch, snoring through a noisy, invariably well-earned nap, his chubby fingers interlaced atop his chubby chest. Laughing like a boy at adolescent jokes on his favorite television shows. Padding from one room to the next, his smile wide, as if he'd just this minute noticed his home, inquiring if dinner was ready.

She could see him in better focus, as someone separate from her, for the first time in years and years.

Because Marianne cocked her eyebrow askance one evening and mentioned that it required more than a comb and brush to make hair presentable, Julia went to Evangeline's and had her hair highlighted. While she was there she asked Evangeline to give her a facial, a skin massage, the expensive works. Because she sensed that Marianne disapproved of her wardrobe, the wardrobe Charles glancingly liked, she went to the third floor of Sherwood's Better department and, taking a deep breath because the bill would eventually be sent home, she ordered three bright dresses she dearly hoped Marianne would approve.

On the main floor, heading for the revolving door, she thought that the pretty girl at the perfume counter, waiting on a bulbous woman, had to be no one but Sally Warner, the girl who had been in the trouble up at Bridgewell Park. She eased her steps and looked. Miss Warner seemed, in the way she moved about, no different from any other girl who never had been improperly handled.

The urge was strong to stop and talk with her, ask her things. But Julia walked on.

Time after time, the meetings with Marianne were almost arrogantly easy to come by. For one reason or another, Marianne's husband was just about never at home, and Charles, for all his good wishes, didn't much notice whether he was left alone or not. They met usually in the evenings, first on Marianne's dimly lighted patio, then on the dark lawn, where the air was fragrantly cool and where the invisible birds sang.

Once, the best time of all, they drove in Marianne's car into the country, far past Underwood, where they were seen only by darting squirrels. The crickets never stopped their chatter. The two women left the car, without a word or even a look, and wandered hand in hand to a south-sloping brook Marianne said she fondly remembered.

They sat at the edge of the brook, listened to its gentle applause, talked together idly yet meaningfully, and then, after waiting too long, Julia was aware of eyes burning into hers and she melted with want. When Marianne touched her endearingly in all those once-dormant, once-secret places, she became tinglingly alive, and Marianne said, "You see? The only time there's an outside world is when we're not together."

Julia was able to tell her everything, everything that ever had been part of her. She told her about the clandestine visit with Dr. Partridge and how, in spite of the ladylike chill she had pretended, she had heard him disclose that what she was doing was in no way wrong.

At last she told her about Mona Vancini, about that brief time at college when she had been both apprehensive and enriched. The experience had made her inexpiably guilty for years afterwards, even after she'd married Charles and, within that presumed safety, she had been satisfied there would never again be temptation.

On that one bouyant and serene day near the brook Marianne had discovered—and wasn't it fantastic that Julia Buckley had been born and raised in Waymouth and never knew there was the brook until Marianne!—they were cozily enclosed by the thrill of Nature, and they shared scandalous and treasured and delicious secrets. They exchanged confidences and Marianne was the true Marianne, not the vulgar, drunkenly cynical person from the Evers Drive of ages ago. They confessed their regrets that they had not found one another long before, in another time, before there had been a Charles Havilland and a Steve Sherwood. For the first unhurried point in their love, they verbalized the depth of their love. Between them, unlike any other couple on earth, there was flawless understanding.

On the unshaven grass, under the vast radiant sky, Marianne rested on her back with her regal head on Julia's lap, and asked Julia to stroke her forehead, to make the small headache go away.

The butterflies were rhythmically polka-dotting the air with their colors. It was the most glorious of days.

"Wouldn't it be perfect if it were like this always?" Julia sighed, gazing out over the water.

"I recall another Julia," Marianne said. "That Julia sat upright in a downright chair and took the affirmative for the solely spiritual life. Ah, she was a stalwart sort."

"Don't tease," Julia laughed. "While we're at it, I recall another Marianne. That Marianne—"

"Please don't remind me. All shell and no egg. Me and my gallant sermons on the joys of unrestricted hedonism and unrestricted drinks."

"What about those drinks?"

"Great Lawdy, do you know something? I haven't even thought of taking a drink since—well, since you and I most poignantly saw the light. Just goes to show you. Love is, how they say, a many-splendored thing."

"I'm so glad. When you're not drinking, you're—"

"Now don't knock drinking. If you hadn't imbibed a bit of the grape yourself, you never would've had the gumption to—"

"Don't, Marianne," Julia interrupted, no longer willing to be frivolous or to endure frivolity. Unconsciously her shoulders straightened for an instant, the only instant that marred the perfect day. "This afternoon let's not be … funny-funny."

"You started it."

"Yes, I know."

Marianne yawned. "Here, today, this is magnificent, isn't it? I feel so contented, so damn happy, that every eternity or so I gawk around to see if I'm allowed to be this happy. You feel that, too?"

"Exactly.

"What did " you say, wouldn't it be nice if things could be like this for us all the time? The answer is a roaring yes. It *would* be nice."

Frowning, Julia said, "You emphasized *would* be nice. I'm not planning to leave for Japan. Are you?"

"I'm not going anywhere. But then neither are Steve or Charles. You talk to me lyrically about idylls and perfection, but now or later, honey, we're going to have to grow up and face the facts. As long as there's a Steve and a Charles, you and I are going to meet like scared thieves."

"Charles is no problem. I fully believe if I were to leave home for a year, he'd add up receipts before he'd think to call for the bloodhounds." Julia said it only because she knew Marianne wanted to hear it, but it didn't come easily. It was gross betrayal talk.

"Is that the time limit you give you and me?" Marianne questioned peevishly. "One year? I grant you, even in the light of day, that forever is a long time, but you and I have discussed forever."

"Oh, I know! I wasn't saying—"

"And I was saying that in life all mistakes ought to be rectified. Unless we're scared thieves, how can you be Charles's and mine both, and how can I be yours and Steve's both?"

"We could murder them," Julia offered, hoping for a chuckle.

"Now I call that impressive judgment. How would we go about it?"

"Let's see. Stilettos are dismally messy ... "

"Actually, we don't have to murder Charles. You said yourself that you'd be the last thing Charles would miss. But Steve would miss me. You are on your way toward gaping down the bodice of a rich gal who doesn't own a dime. If we murder Steve, though—and I can't imagine anyone easier to murder—and if he's murdered with the proper decorum, then the widder lady inherits bushels and bushels of moolah, and you and I sail out, as interwoven as a plate of spaghetti, to Bermuda or Haiti, where we live like royalty forever. 'Forever.' Who's word was that? Yours or mine?"

"Honestly, Marianne, I wish I had your sense of fantasy."

"Yeah. It's some buster, isn't it?"

It was the most precious of days, limitlessly finer than the day she had spent walking at the rim of the river with Mona, if only because she had known torpid, hideous guilt then and felt absolutely none now.

Finally the ardent sun winked that it was preparing to lower, and, after neither of them had felt compelled to say a word for stretched minutes, Marianne arched slightly and rose to lean on an elbow. She studied Julia's face, quizzically, as though she intended to memorize every line and plane of it.

"The headache's disappeared," she stated in an ominously terse voice. "Shall we dance?"

Julia had no intention of ever seeing Dr. Partridge again, but she had two demonic dreams, two nights in a row, dreams which in each case roused her sharply out of sleep, in a bath of perspiration. Charles, who slept like the dead, was immediately at the side of his bed each time, ready to hasten to her. Each time she took gurgling, almost convulsive gasps of breath as she sat up, but each time she soon relaxed and, seeing Charles's grave concern, rejoined life and assured him she had been silly and had eaten the wrong things before going to bed.

The dreams made so little sense that, by morning, she remembered them not at all, but the shakiness remained tenaciously, long after she'd bathed and dressed. Because, along about mid-afternoon, she had vivid recollections that their feeling tone, if not their story line, dealt with Mona and Marianne, she thrashed about the house endlessly. When her attention span on almost every idea or object lessened to interrupted seconds, she telephoned the number. Guaranteed anonymity as she had been granted before, she asked for an early appointment with Dr. Partridge.

Much less brittle with him than she had been the first time
she had come to him, Julia parried for only half the hour with
inconsequentials and then explained—purposely holding his eye
as she dove with all her wits into the assuredly rough waters—
that as he may or may not know it, and it couldn't matter less to
her, she was unhamperedly involved with a woman who lived in
Waymouth.

"Unhampered?" he said. "If you're unhampered, Mrs.
Havilland, why did you ask to see me again?"

It was a vicious question, but it was a good question, too. She
gave herself the luxury of composure before she answered him.

"I've been having these frightful dreams," she replied. "I've
never had bad dreams, let alone any dreams at all, at night, ever in
my life." She pretended he was totally disembodied, an adequate
form with nothing but ears, and, devoid of passion, she released
everything she had not released the first time here, about Mona
Vancini and about Marianne.

"You're telling me, Mrs. Havilland, not asking me," the
snip remarked. "Obviously you're guilty about something. If
you're asking something, what are you asking? Is your present
affair justified, right, normal? To all those questions, the answer
is an unqualified yes. You're a perfectly normal woman, Mrs.
Havilland. Is there anything else to discuss?"

At home, the positive rightness retreated into the shadows,
and Julia entertained the idea for full minutes at a time of drawing Charles away from his work to confide that she felt lost.
Viewing him at his desk, the word "lost" shot back to her brain
and sounded outrageously melodramatic. They had been married a great many years and, for all his natural gifts, Charles was
always abjectly startled by melodrama.

Julia kept going to Marianne, with a consuming desire, every
time both of them were free. Infrequently the talk about murder
occurred to her, but, for the most part, only in passing. She was
alarmed when, at one terrible moment, Marianne turned to her

in the darkness of the Evers Drive garden and asked her, "Have you done any thinking about what we discussed at the brook? About Steve?"

The lilt was not in her voice.

"We have so little time," said Julia. "Let's not waste it with little jokes."

"I love you, Julia, and I want to see the two of us out there, forever and ever, in some warm place like Bermuda. Do you love me?"

"Oh, yes!"

"Then answer me here and now. As long as I'm Steve's wife, you and I will be nothing but alley cats. If Steve's gone, you and I will be what we were meant to be. I'll ask you once more. Do you love me?"

"Yes. You know I do. But..."

"If Steve's done away with, you and I can be happier than we possibly could be in Waymouth, here in the shadows, sneaking about like pack rats. I'm talking sense, honey. We love each other so much that you can pause for a breath and I know what you want to say. Life hits us just once and then never again. You can leave Charles any time you choose. I want Steve out of the way because I want you. It couldn't be simpler. Are you with me?"

"Marianne, the way you talk..."

"Life hits us once, and only once. The merry-go-round never quite repeats the same song. Are you with me for the ride or do you want to see the gold ring from the sidelines?"

"If I could only..."

"Is it a deal?"

At her counter near the front of the store, Sally Warner waited on a querulous woman who wanted Chanel No. 6. Sally told her that the Chanels stopped at 5, but the woman insisted she had read that a Chanel No. 6 was on the market. When Sally quietly disagreed, the woman demanded to see someone in charge.

Miss Raines, her section manager, instructed her at fifteen minutes before closing that she was wanted in Mr. Sherwood's office.

"Mr. Lawrence or Mr. Steven?" Sally asked guardedly, praying that the secret was not reflected in her face or voice. In the two and a half years she had worked here, neither Sherwood, father or son, had called her to the second-floor offices.

"Mr. Steven."

His office, next to his father's was at the rear of the long second floor, past the men's furnishings and the account windows. His secretary, whom she recognized as one of the Ciamino girls who lived off Griswold Street, came out of the office and nodded for her to go right in.

Brusquely he told her to close the door and pretended more brusqueness until she obeyed and he appeared sure they could neither be seen nor heard. He didn't bother to rise but his smile broadened, in a sort of almost lewd intimacy which disturbed and displeased her.

"I have some news for you, Miss Warner. You don't mind if I call you Miss Warner during working hours. Sit down."

Sally sat in the chair beside his desk.

"I was intending to keep the information to myself for a while," he said, "at least, say, until this weekend, when you and I fly up to Preston's Landing. I was going to spring it on you there, but I think you'll agree it's a little too good to keep."

"Preston's … I'm afraid I'm not following you … "

Steven's smile remained broad, but it had imperceptibly become impish, and faintly self-conscious. "On Friday at six you're going to meet me at the corner of Cosgrove, and we'll drive to the airport. We can be at the Landing in an hour. The sailing there is ideal and I've doped out equally ideal names for us: Mr. and Mrs. H. J. Howard. How does that sound, being Mrs. H. J. Howard for a full weekend?"

She was unsure of what she saw, but she thought the smile had descended to a smirk. This strange kind of souped-up talk was not in keeping with him. He looked as he had looked an instant before their first meaningful kiss, when she had so completely received him, but now he had added the two bad ingredients, smirk and self-consciousness, and she was sorry he had wanted her to see him this way.

"That's—quite an invitation, Steven," she said, almost afraid to meet his eyes.

"Here's the news. You can give it some thought while you're packing summer things. Your section manager's leaving at the end of the month for a two-week vacation. My father hired her a hundred and seventy-seven years ago and nobody's thought to let her go even though she's at the retirement age. The point is that I'm letting her go, the day she comes back. I'd have one of the staff tell her so before she takes off, but why spoil her vacation?"

"If you want an opinion, Miss Raines will be doing her job as well for the next hundred and seventy-seven years."

"That's possible. But it's also just as possible that you can do it even better."

"Me? In Miss Raines's job?"

"You know the department from A to Z."

"But—"

"And the salary is considerably higher." Because he noticed the questioning look she gave him, his smirk switched to the smile. "Let's not go into any deep discussion about it here and now," he said. "I'll see that all the details are handled, and we can talk about it at leisure up at the Landing. All right? Now I guess you'd better go. I gave my secretary a cock-and-bull story about why I wanted to see you, and it wouldn't pay to have rumors circulated, would it? Actually, I just wanted to see you, Sally, see you up close. I've had you on my mind all day. I have a meeting tonight or I would've blown your door down and made you see me."

"Steven, we should talk..."

"I suppose I have one of those boomerang personalities. I was cool on the way home from the motel. You sensed it; I'm positive you did. I needed time to get a full picture of you. Well, I've had the time. You're special to me, Sally, and I'd do just about anything to keep from losing you. You believe that, don't you?"

She went home the next evening to find her father and Frances sitting at the dining-room table. The table had not been set for dinner. The waxed fruit was still in the lumpy glass bowl in the direct center.

Will Warner glared at her and she felt as she had felt numberless times before, unsettled and curiously undressed. Over the last few slanting years he had become small in size, incredibly old. His eyebrows had burgeoned into gray bushes and his once-powerful hands were now wrinkled and pathetic puffballs. Consumed in hate and blindness and the inability to wholly love anything, he was old and he never would be young again.

"You was a whore in the park and I protected you because you was my daughter," he said evenly. "But now you're a whorelady for good and all, and as God is my witness you're not my daughter any longer."

"Pa, please," Frances said and touched his elbow. "You promised you wouldn't—"

His voice lifted as he brushed her hand away, his attention glued to Sally. "I ordered you a thousand and one times, I'm the man in this household and no one's ever to say 'please' to me!"

Frances was still.

"Nobody ever changes the leopard's spots," he declared. "A store thief stays a store thief, a lady stays a lady like your sister Frances Jane and her mother before her, God rest her heavenly soul, and a whorelady stays a whorelady. It wasn't enough you was a whorelady in Bridgewell Park with that school teacher and that maniac wop. You had to do better. You had to go with all the rest of the whores up the hill to that sinful place where that band of niggers and Jew-kikes make you tell them sinful words for their sex survey and I have dollars to doughnuts that says you showed them in person how good a whorelady you can be when you set your filthy little mind to it."

Sally stood erect in front of the yellow flowered wallpaper and tried to assure herself the day had been rattled and that she would wake up. This was insane talk, even for him, and she wished the desperately unmoored feeling would leave.

"I've had a hard day at the store," she volunteered, hoping she could get away with it, "and I don't understand what you're saying. I'll have a bath and a change, and I'll come down and we can—"

"You'll have nothing else again in my house!" he roared and charged at her. From an inch away his pathetic hand lifted and slapped her cheek. "If you stay in my house a minute longer than it takes you to rid my house of your belongings, I swear I'll pull my Luger out of my top drawer and get your dirty brains shot out of your head! Ray Edson seen you twittering your little backside into that sinful place, young whorelady. Yes, Ray Edson, my oldest friend from The Grandsons of Bull Run! And he went and told Chubby Walter and Vance Harley and Mitch Young, the best friends I ever had, and now what am I but one of your whorelady laughingstocks? I got rights, I got the finest name there is in Waymouth, and the likes of you ain't going to keep them hurt. You killed my wife, but you sure as hell ain't going to ruin me!"

Sally looked at Frances, but Frances sat immobile at her place, blinking helplessly at her hands.

"Get out of my house," said Will Warner. "In a week or two weeks or three weeks, maybe I'll have a change of heart, but you can bet your bottom dollar I got no call to be wheedled now. I see you when I come home from work in the morning, I'll kill you like you killed my wife."

As far as she could judge, he hadn't had one drink.

At the corner of Griswold Street, holding an overnight bag, Sally wondered where she was to go next. She thought of Dr. Morrow and of Steven Sherwood, but she could not bring herself to go to either of them. She thought of the people who might put her up for the night, passed over Guv Barnes, and remembered Eileen Page, the girl she had graduated from high school with, the girl who had married Ronnie Shepherd, Sally's very first boy friend who now worked at Arbrought's, the girl who'd once advised, "If you ever need a pair of Trojan pals, here we are."

She went to the candy store at Cosgrove and Eighth, ashamed of the bag she carried, and stepped into the telephone booth, ready to dig for Eileen and Ronnie's number. When she realized that she would be expected to come up with some sort of explanation, Trojan pals or no Trojan pals, she retreated from the booth.

Her head felt numb. She leafed through the pages of the telephone book, found the number of The Hotel Waymouth, and dialed it. She asked for Dr. Philip Morrow, was asked her name, gave it, and within a minute heard him answer. His voice was instantly, undeniably concerned. She was convinced that Steven's would have been clouded.

"May I see you, Dr. Morrow? Tonight?"

"You sound urgent."

"May I see you?"

"Certainly. You name the place. I'll be here, waiting, or you suggest something else and I'll be there in minutes."

"Where you are . .. will you be alone?"

"I'll see that I am."

"I'll be there soon," she said.

Paying strict attention to everything she said, Phil was positive that she was only secondarily upset by her father's lashing out and ordering her from his house. Sherwood was the main attraction. The taken-for-granted attitude that she would fly away with him for the weekend, the smirkingly swinish minor blackmail about firing the section manager and hiring her to take the woman's place, announcing it hand-in-hand with the announcement of the flight. The experience with Barnes, by comparison, had been an innocent romp in the woods.

They sat in the suite's living room and he regarded her, a helpless waif who trusted him because there seemed no one else on earth left to trust.

"Your father would have found another alibi for throwing his sad weight around, if we'd come to Waymouth or if we hadn't," Phil offered. "Maybe he wouldn't have gone so far as he did tonight, but at least it clears the air, doesn't it? A mature father never behaves that way, no matter what his daughter's done, certainly not if she's indicated her need for a father as often as you've indicated it to him. You knew that something would have to come to a head with him, sooner or later. Otherwise, you'd coast along and become Frances in time. You implied as much during our interview."

"I—kept hoping," she said falteringly, "that something would make him change. Maybe Bob's death and what happened to me that night. I hoped that in time he'd be what he'd been when I was a child."

"But that's a dream, too, isn't it? Was he a better father when you were a child?"

Sally looked at the window behind him, paused, and then slowly shook her head.

"When I was very young he'd be good to me in the mornings. I'd live for those mornings. He'd nuzzle his nose into my neck and make me giggle, and he'd swing me around and tickle my stomach and my knees. He'd tell me to keep it a big, dark secret, but that he loved me more than he loved Frances. I suppose I knew even then that it was a bad thing to say, but I believed it and I was sure he meant it.

"Those were the mornings he'd be feeling fine," she went on. "We had a housekeeper then, when he still had his store and before Frances was old enough to take care of the house and go to school both. She was a German woman we called Gussa, and I don't think I ever suspected there was anything between her and my father until I was a lot older. Somebody began a rumor that he kept Gussa there at the house for—you know. I don't see any reason why the rumor couldn't be true…

"Anyway, he'd always promise to bring me a gift when he came home, a doll house or a puppy or, oh, something different every time. I'd wait all day. Some nights he wouldn't come home at all. When he did come home he'd be altogether different. He'd be angry, or he wouldn't say a word to any of us. Sometimes he'd be very drunk. I'd ask him about the present, and he either wouldn't even look at me, or he'd slap me, for no reason at all. Then, after a while, he wasn't so nice to me in the mornings, and then he began that talk about my killing his wife."

"So his being a good father when you were small… that was mostly fantasy, wasn't it? The truth is that your father *never* had anything for you."

She nodded.

"And then you grew up and went to a park at night with your fiance, and the love he was about to give you was interrupted. Again you were stalled, again you were told you were entitled to nothing. For the first time you recognized the impasse and in a frantic way, as if you'd wasted too much time already and because you couldn't admit that you'd never have a father who was capable of love and protectiveness, you rushed out and tried to invent one. Isn't that what happened, Sally?"

Tears glistened in her eyes, but she neither nodded nor shook her head. Phil waited and let her know by his silence that he understood that she had heard him and taken in something of what he had said.

"Sally," he pointed out tenderly, "wasn't it Steven Sherwood who really offended you yesterday? The vulgar casualness of his invitation? After all these years with your father, nothing he said or did could wound you except momentarily. But Sherwood is new to you. At the beginning he was kind and good, the way your father was kind and good in the mornings. What kind of love did Sherwood offer you yesterday? The old, stale, selfish kind. Loveless and cold."

Timidly she attempted to correct him, but almost abruptly dropped it. "Last night in bed," she conceded, "I had no feeling for him, but I planned to go away with him. I thought that I'd misunderstood the way he'd talked to me, that up at Preston's Landing he'd change, he'd—be what I hoped for."

"Your thoughts went beyond Preston's Landing, didn't they? If he turned out to be Guv Barnes all over again, what did you plan to do next?"

"I was going to find someone else." She looked squarely at Phil. "And then someone else after that."

"Of course. The night in the park served as a trigger. With some screwy sort of arithmetic, you were going to seek out two or six or eight half-men who would add up to one whole man."

"Yes."

"It's not only lousy arithmetic, Sally," he asserted, and his smile was direct, "it's lousy sense."

Over the next half-hour, until he was convinced her major anxieties had lessened for the time being, he did not mention Steven Sherwood's name. He exacted no promises from her. When he remembered that he had an avalanche of work ahead of him, he asked her if there was a hotel nearby where she would be comfortable for the night or for the next several nights, until she became settled away from home and decided on where she would move. She caught his omitting the suggestion of his own hotel, caught the nuance of what would be unfortunately inferred if she were invited to sleep under the same overall roof. He was pleased that she in no way played it up.

After thinking for a moment, she said, "There's a nice hotel called The Bromley, about halfway between here and where I work." Phil telephoned there, made a reservation for her, and offered to lend ten dollars to tide her over till pay day. She did not want to accept the loan but, when he asked her how much she had in her purse, confessed that she had little cash.

Returning to his work after Sally Warner left, Phil thought about her intermittently, and occasionally for long consecutive minutes at a stretch. He regretted that they hadn't met under less confining circumstances.

CHAPTER SIX

❧ ❧ ❧

URDER, THOUGHT Julia Havilland, was something you read about in the tabloids. Stumblebums murdered other stumblebums on Skid Row for pennies and for canned heat. Addicts murdered doctors for supplies of dope. Angry people murdered angry people for angry reasons.

Decent human beings discovered other means of solving their vital problems.

On the day that Marianne bluntly gave her two alternatives, either they did away with Steve or there would be no more meetings, Julia knew finally that the joking, wistful conversations were over and that she now could no more give up Marianne than she could swim to Europe. Driving back home after one perfectly exquisite evening in the blackness of Marianne's lawn, summoning old, familiar poems and revealing new, unfamiliar delights, she tried to dredge up memories of what had thrilled her before she had been so totally wakened by Marianne. She recalled only the passing ecstacy of Mona Vancini, and the infrequent pleasure of being the wife of Waymouth's most successful realtor. In the next few breaths she would be forty. A breath later she would be fifty and then sixty. She could not die with such a lack of fulfillment.

The sight of Charles became unwholesome and the expectation of living out the remainder of her years with him intolerable.

She saw young Dr. Partridge, for all his brashness, more and more as an unquestionable authority. She knew Marianne as the only honest love of her dreary life, the one love that made existence possible.

"It's a ridiculously foolproof plan," Marianne said. "I couldn't ever have thought it up if I hadn't been lucky enough to meet you. If you'd stayed where you belonged, down there safely tucked away on Northrop Street with all your charming committees, I would have dragged along as Mrs. Hausfrau till death us did part. The plan is crystal clear now, though. The last time we've had a burglary of any size here on Evers Drive was, as I remember, shortly before the firing on Fort Sumter, but we have a reputation here of inviting small robberies. Everybody Steve knows knows he loves this backyard garden. During the summer, and I guess even during the fall, he walks around here for a while the night's last pipe. As sure as the Chambord has celebrities, he'll arrive Thursday night and walk his grounds like that dour man from Jane Eyre. I own a loaded pistol. I weep and wail for the police. My husband saw fit to stay away on most nights because of business, and I'm nervous, and when I saw this man prowling around I went to him and he shouted to me and before I knew what I was doing, I killed him."

"But, Marianne," pleaded Julia, "how do I come into it?"

"It's simple. You're my dearest friend, you're Waymouth's Mrs. Havilland. You agreed to stay the night with me because my husband's business hours were so erratic that I gradually got frightened at night. You heard me leave my room and you got up to help me back to bed. When I kept going, you followed me. You saw me shoot my own husband and you were horror-stricken. When I realized my mistake, you did your level best to comfort me."

"Marianne—"

"Does all this suddenly shock you? Let me know, honey, please. I've planned it all for only one reason: I want money and freedom enough to leave this sinkhole and get us a one-way fare to Haiti. I've told you about that heavenly place. If you have the vaguest objections, let me know now, and I'll switch off all the lights."

"The lights…"

"If they're switched off, then you and I are switched off, too, honey. Steve knows about us. Maybe I shouldn't put it in such bold letters. In his woebegone wisdom, he suspects. I've spoken about you too highly, too often. He's as tightlipped as can be—that's a Sherwood tradition. But I know he suspects something close and wonderful is going on. Before long he's going to call my hand. If we don't put him out of the way soon, there'll never be another chance for you and me. If we do, though—skillfully, cleanly, without any unnecessary histrionics—then I stay here for a decent length of time after it's all over, until everyone says 'There goes poor Widow Sherwood; how pale and lost she looks!' and until I collect the money that's due me. You'll be with me to corroborate the story. You're the safety valve, don't you see? You're Mrs. Havilland, and no one points an accusing finger at Mrs. Havilland or at Mrs. Havilland's friends. We can take off for anywhere in the world within months, and stay there for the rest of our lives. No one will miss us."

Julia felt heady and powerless as she murmured, "There's Charles…"

"Yes, there's Charles," Marianne snapped in an alarmingly mocking tone. "I'm giving up Steve and my home here because I want you. What are you saying? That you want me but that you aren't prepared to sacrifice anything or anybody?"

She was adrift everytime Marianne snapped at her. Marianne had spoken persuasively about the world outside Waymouth, where there was peace and love. Why was she so harsh now?

"We're not pigtailed adolescents, Julia, telling ouurselves we'll find the bluebird when we turn eighteen. We've turned eighteen and we either start looking out for ourselves or we accept the fact that ruts are permanent and we go back to our rocking chairs."

"I couldn't bear not seeing you again," Julia breathed and, suddenly cold, fled to her for warmth.

For a time she was safe and all that was evil was blotted from her mind. Then with jolting speed it was Thursday evening and Charles rose from the dinner table and rubbed his napkin at his lips. He would have just time enough to go over his work in the study before his shows began on television at 7:30, he said. On his way from the room he passed her chair and patted her shoulder. "That baked halibut's a real treat, Julia," he acknowledged. "Let's have it again soon."

The telephone rang and she darted for it so quickly that Charles chuckled and told her not to forget to touch second base.

"Hello, Julia," she heard. "This is Marianne. Would you be free to drop over tonight? I'm sure I sound like a silly old woman, but I've heard there are prowlers around Evers Drive these evenings, and even with the servants here I've been tiptoeing about, peeking under beds and inside closets. Would you mind terribly keeping me company till Steve gets home?"

When the almost curtly efficient phone call came in, advising her that the Alders surveyors had gone over her interview, had concluded that they had more than enough information and thank you very much, Marianne was sure there was some mistake. They had mixed up her interview with someone else's. Dr. Crayne had assured her he wanted to see her again, hadn't he?

"May I talk with Dr. Crayne, please?"

"I'm sorry, Mrs. Sherwood," came the resonant voice. "Dr. Crayne cannot be disturbed."

First Marianne had an urge to see if she could yank the telephone from the wall, and then thought that no one would ring for the Black Maria if she simply sat down and had a good, old-fashioned weeping binge.

She did neither. Without warning, she began to laugh. She walked the length and breadth of the house's second floor and the unrestrained, boisterous laughter poured voluptuously from her. She went to the accordion closet in her bedroom, took down the bottle of "In-Case" brandy, drank ravenously, and laughed some more.

Hurry, hurry, hurry, folks, she called, step right up and inspect the human pincushion. Bring your own pins and try your luck. Satisfaction guaranteed. References on request. Aaron Miles, Dan Parrish, the whole goddamn kiboodle. And now the grand finale. The saga of my sex life doesn't even rate an encore. "Come back with more, Marianne. Are you all ready to come back? Okay, I've changed my mind. Take six giant steps backwards and sit in a corner."

Laugh here.

She capped the bottle and replaced it when she remembered that this was no day in which to be squiffed. Later, again and again and again later, but not now. Back in California, with her friends, the kids who demanded nothing from her except that she be herself, she would be in the happy thick of good drinking weather. You could always tie one on in Beverly Hills far more fancily and with far less recrimination than on the East Coast. And this time she would be swinging back there with a pot of gold. Alone, a widow, cascading money, she wouldn't get lost. Not ever again.

She called the store and asked to speak with Steve. Thursday was advertising night, when he and his father and Steiner and King holed themselves up in an office to plan the next week's newspaper layouts. If he didn't have other personal fish to fry on Thursday nights, he came home by half-past ten.

Steve was surprised to hear her voice.

"Will you be home tonight right after you leave your conference?" she inquired without a semblance of bite.

"I didn't know you cared."

"Please, Steve, don't rake me over the coals now. I suppose I sound like a silly old woman, but I'm just a little bit uneasy."

"Uneasy? What's wrong, Marianne?"

"Oh, it's stupid, I know, but I've been hearing reports of a prowler scooting around in the district. Mrs. Quigley and the maid are going to be in, but I'd—well, I'll shame the devil and say it, Steve. I'd feel better if you were here with me."

"You're kidding, aren't you?"

"You know I'm not much of a kidder."

The line seemed dead for a few seconds, and then he said, "You sound as though you mean it, at that. Let me see. I can skip the ad meeting and come home right away."

"No, no, no, I wouldn't hear of that. I'll be perfectly all right. All I meant was that I'd appreciate it if—if you'd spend the night with me, Steve."

She waited for him to either try to pursue what she was saying, after years of snarls and silences, or to readily accede. As she expected, he acceded. He promised to be home by half-past ten.

It took consummate genius to be skillful with Mrs. Quigley, but she was positive she could swing it. She told the housekeeper that she had phoned Mr. Sherwood and he had said he wouldn't be home tonight. She added that it was a little spooky, wasn't it? that prowlers were in the neighborhood. The cloddish woman grunted that she hadn't heard any such thing. Marianne started to leave the room and then, dramatically, turned.

"Have you noticed anything odd about Mrs. Havilland lately?" she asked, working to both proclaim and courageously mask her pretense of deep concern.

"Odd? Can't say's I have, any more than usual."

"She's coming to visit me again tonight. I wish she wouldn't. I'm a little—frightened of her, Mrs. Quigley."

The housekeeper frowned. "What's going on with you? I never seen you so worried looking."

"Maybe you could tell her when she comes that I'm out. I don't want to see her. Possibly you can—oh, no, forget it. I wouldn't want you to say anything that wasn't true."

"You all right, Mrs. Sherwood?"

"I—hope so," Marianne replied and purposely walked away with an impression left in the air that she was gravely troubled.

Less than half an hour before Julia was expected, Marianne took the pistol from the inside pocket of an old camel's-hair coat she kept in one of the storage closets, packed its tissue paper more tightly around the gun, and dug it into the deep pocket of her skirt. She decided to help herself to one more snort from the bottle, although she felt equitably calm, almost tranquil.

Descending the stairway, she went over the story once more and was delighted by its fluidity.

"I didn't know Mrs. Havilland very well," she would tell the police between carefully organized hysterics. Maybe there would be a roster of photographers on hand. "We had very little in common, but I'd let her visit me now and then because she seemed so lonely. She kept complaining about her husband, about how negligent he was of her. I began as a sounding board for her because I took pity on her. Then—I have no idea how it came up, what prompted it—one night she made an improper advance to me. I imagine I give the effect of sophistication to people here in Waymouth, but what she did shocked me. I told her that if there was ever anything more like that, our friendship was at an end.

"She apologized but she begged to see me again. She gave me her word it would never happen again. I sensed how lonely she must have been, so I let her come back.

"She misunderstood my sympathy because, before I knew it, things got out of hand. She became almost like a lunatic. She raved and cried and said she was in love with me, that she couldn't stand the thought of my husband touching me. This was a few nights ago. I told her to leave. I told her that if she didn't leave me alone I'd tell her husband and my own husband how she was behaving.

"Tonight she said she was coming back. I told her I wouldn't be home, but she came anyway. I was going to have it out with her, once and for all, but then she began talking crazy talk, mad talk, about how she'd been living a lie all these years, incoherent talk. I was...fearful. Then my husband came out on the patio and all of a sudden she was taking a gun from her purse. I still couldn't believe she was so overwrought that she'd do anything so mad. I tried to stop her, called for my husband to run away. But it was too late. She—"

Oh, it was magnificent, thought Marianne, feeling ideally relaxed and fully in charge of herself. Every newspaper in the country, in the world, will write about it. About Marianne Terrin. They'll dig into the files and come up with the beautiful Flatow pictures of me, the ones he took during *Sons of Solomon,* the pictures of me that won all those prizes.

What's that, my dear? You say Mr. Aaron Miles is on the line and wishes to speak with me? He desires to discuss my playing the title role in *Lot's Wife?* Thank you, my dear, but will you kindly tell Mr. Aaron. Miles to go lay an egg, the kind of egg his picture will lay? I need Mr. Aaron Miles like I need Asian flu.

They're all after me now, my dear Mr. Miles's loyal toady, waving those fat contracts in my face. Yes, my beautiful face, the face that hasn't changed an iota in ten years.

I don't need you. I don't need anyone, not the acceptance of Dr. Crayne, not anyone.

I am Marianne Terrin. Paste that in your bonnet. I am going to be the greatest star that ever lived. Again.

Steve Sherwood said goodbye to Marianne, replaced the receiver, and felt a gnawing frustration because he couldn't go to her immediately. Her call, tinged with the subtlest yet most unmistakable come-on, was like old times. She wanted to be his wife. He wanted to be with her, but he was almost grateful that she'd turned down his offer to skip the ad meeting. Dad had been riding him pretty hard about missing those meetings, dull as dishwater as they were, and this wasn't the time to send Dad off on the Sherwood warpath.

The good thing about the call was that it came when it did. This afternoon Sally Warner had asked to see him in private. In this office she had stood at a distance from his desk and, talking in a tremulous voice but not really batting an eye, had informed him she would not go away with him this weekend, or any weekend. She would not see him again on any intimate basis. If he wanted to discharge her, that was his right.

Her ultimatum tone annoyed him as it made him lonely, made him think of the future and see nothing in store but negotiations with his list of madames, the last outpost of the unneeded man. He demanded to know what all the hifalutin' foolishness was about. She answered it was complicated, but that she couldn't go on with something she knew was terribly wrong. Because she stood there like an employer, issuing orders to the stockroom boy, he was damned if he would coax or whine or wheedle. Curtly he notified her that she was to understand the project of replacing Miss Raines was not quite out of the question. She seemed unfazed as she nodded. He told her to get back to her counter.

The rejection stung. He had intended to live it up with her for certainly another week, possibly even longer, and her turning him down, after what he'd given her and was promising to give her, was both uncalled for and hurtful. But then Marianne's call lightened the hurt. From the time he had met Marianne she had used him and gone out of her way to pin his ears back, but he'd always known that one day she would come to her senses and realize that they still could pick up the pieces and make a meaningful marriage. Maybe he was grabbing for straws again. Maybe she was just being her ornery capricious self, but somehow he doubted it. She wasn't that accomplished an actress. She had been sincere and forthright on the telephone, and it had been ages since he'd recognized anything like that in her.

At 8:30, after dinner with Dad at The Waymouthite, where Dad's talk shuttled between the business and veiled snipes at Marianne, the advertising meeting commenced, and Steve was restless for it to be over. By ten o'clock, when everyone but Dad agreed to adjourn, the urge to race home was stronger than it had been in years.

On the way home, he considered the two plane tickets and his reservation at Preston's Landing. There was no reason to cancel them. Sally Warner could stay home and bite her fingernails, regretting what she had passed up. He would take Marianne with him. Mr. and Mrs. Steven Sherwood. He would encourage her to take along one of her scandalous bathing suits, the kind that showed everyone how impeccably built his still youthful wife was. Someone would remember her from when she'd been on the screen, or they would pretend to. Marianne would eat that up. She had been in only two pictures, and in supporting roles at that, but she was a purring kitten when anyone remembered her as a movie actress.

At night they would go dancing and, because she'd know again that heavy drinking had no place in honeymoons, she would limit herself to one drink or, at the most, two. They wouldn't require any words to know it was time to go back to their room. There they would take a lingering shower together. She would whisper to him and they would make love through the night, as they once had done, feverishly and then with caressing gentleness.

The ugly times would be forgotten. They would be man and wife again, as they had meant and fundamentally always wanted to be.

Steve drove the car into the garage beneath the house, stepped out, and ascended the rock stairs which led to the patio and back yard, where he thought he heard her. The only light came from inside the house. But that, surely, had been intentional on her part, too. One summer night, long ago, he had found her in the yard. He had just begun to ask her why she was waiting for him in the dark when he touched her and knew she was naked. He had needed to say nothing more.

He saw her now, standing at the other end of the yard near the rose bushes. Walking swiftly over the lightly damp grass, he raised his arms to her and was bewildered to see that the woman was not his Marianne, but someone else, someone he only dimly recognized. He slackened his steps an instant before he heard Marianne, indisputably Marianne, call out, "Now! Do it now!"

"Marianne?" he said.

The woman who was not his wife retreated in some sort of staggering fright, and he saw Marianne leap at her and force the woman's hand from her side. When the woman would not move and he had the sick feeling that she held a gun, he stood tall and wondered why his legs would not let him run away. He heard Marianne cry, "You stinking bitch! Give me that!" and then he faced the object in Marianne's hand and heard a sharp noise and felt a stunning pain in his chest.

His Marianne was coming toward him, her face contorted in hate, and she shot him again and then again. His hands were paralyzed but his legs were water as he stood far, far away and watched Steven Sherwood slither to the lawn.

A moment ago the patio he had shared with Marianne had been dark, but now it was uncommonly bright with light. The house was lighted and the whole sky was vivid with light. He heard screams and then he heard nothing, but he still saw the fierce, all-beholding light.

He started to ask Marianne why, but all the lights were switched off.

❧ ❧ ❧

When she entered the lobby of The Bromley to check in, Sally slackened her steps, but it was too late to turn and run away. Old Mr. Kinkaid recognized her. Mr. Kinkaid, the hotel's night desk clerk, had taught her American history at Waymouth High a half-dozen years ago, the year he'd been retired. His eyesight was failing and he doddered, but he nodded to her and she knew he remembered her.

He had been her favorite high-school teacher then, largely because he had taken a paternal fancy to her. He had complimented her on her compositions and her alertness in class, as the other teachers had not. The other kids had seen him as something of a relic because he'd worn high collars, a string necktie, and those Abraham Lincoln shoes, but Sally had had a minor crush on him, as she'd always suspected he had on her.

Facing him now, checking into a local hotel late at night, she felt worn and sleazy.

"Your room's ready for you, Sally," he said as she went through the dreadful formality of signing her name and address. "Second floor front. Buster over there'll take you up. Maybe you recollect Buster Granger. The two of you were in my history class."

"Yes," she nodded. "Thank you, Mr. Kinkaid."

In the room, Sally took a long hot bath, fully intending to sink into the double bed and drop immediately off to sleep, assured that tomorrow would take care of itself.

Twisting about, an hour later, fighting gnarled sheets and blankets, she knew that sleep was impossible. At one point she sat upright in the lone bed, switched on the light, and was harassed when she recognized why sleep, which she had always been able to summon with fair ease, would not come.

Hating herself, she left the bed and dressed again decisively. Not bothering to glance at the time, or ponder the consequences, she walked out of the hotel room, slipped down the corridor, and descended the back stairs of The Bromley to the street. She kept walking, until she reached Lassiterville. She had heard that Lassiterville never closed up, that action prevailed at any hour of the night if action was desired.

The long and dark walk to the side roads of Lassiterville took, surprisingly, little more than half an hour, circuitous routes and all. She had a distant recollection of Guv Barnes, the fantasy of seeing him here in all his cruelty, waiting for her, suspended in time.

The first bar Sally entered was called Siggie's Domain, and it was more crowded than she would have thought. A cluster of men, in either sports shirts or scarred leather jackets, were crouched in the vicinity of the single bartender, and most of them were looking up at the wrestling match on the television set perched high over the clock. At the rear sat one woman, a veiny woman with lemon-colored hair, well into her forties, deep in conversation with an astonishingly old man who appeared to hang on her every word. He reminded Sally of her father, a man who belonged home in bed.

The horrendous thought, *fish out of water,* occurred to Sally as she stepped up to the bar and asked for a glass of beer. But the need, the dreary yet overpowering need, would not leave.

Presently, one of the men in leather jackets sidled up to her and grinned. She grinned back, holding in her nervousness. He was young, perhaps in his middle twenties, and, except for at least one broken tooth and whitish cheeks, he was no different from the line of other men at the bar.

"What're you, this time of night?" he asked. "The thirsty type? A big-deal beer guzzler?"

"What's wrong with beer?"

"What's wrong with a walk around the block?"

"Not a thing," said Sally.

"Let's finish up, in a hurry, and then there's that back door, right behind you. You know where it's at?"

"Why are you all of a sudden trembling?" she teased.

"You know where it's at, or you want to keep on talking snotty?"

"I'll finish in a minute. Should we go out together, or should I meet you there?"

"Yeah, that's a great idea. You go right outside and you'll see a Quinn truck in the lot. That's mine." He recited the license plate number. "I'll see you in just a couple minutes."

Obediently, Sally set her beer on the bar and left the long, narrow room for the darkened lot. The truck was not hard to find. He appeared sooner than she would have suspected, and directed, "Let's see what we see in the back row. You ready?"

"The back row?" she questioned.

"Through the back," he rasped, and led her to the rear of the truck. She stepped up the three short bars into the musty truck, and smelled something fruity, probably oranges.

In the near dark, Sally sat at the very rear of the empty truck and watched him hover, fussing with his belt buckle.

"I sure never saw you around here before," he said.

"I—didn't hear your name."

"Name? You need a name? John Smith. You got a name?"

"Mary Smith."

"Glad to meet'cha," he laughed. "It's a wild day when John Smith meets Mary Smith."

Through glazed eyes Sally saw the olive-green chinos dropped to the floor of the truck. She thought of Dr. Morrow and of their time together, but the man who called himself John Smith interrupted.

"Let's go to work, babe," he said. "I got to pull out for downstate in a little while."

"Honey .. ".

"What?"

"I'm going to make the strangest request you've ever had."

"Which is?" he asked, cocking a bushy eyebrow.

"Don't be tender," said Sally. "Be masculine, be vicious. Treat me the way your instincts tell you to treat me. Whatever you do, don't be kind."

He cooperated.

"You're wearing too many clothes," he said.

"I am?"

"Get them off. Quick."

Sally complied.

The man leapt on her with a ferocious cry and took her with a speed which alarmed her. Only when he was through did he speak to her. He inquired: "How you doin'?"

"Fine."

"I got to go soon. See you around sometime?"

Sally didn't answer.

Rising onto his elbow, he was angry. "When I put a question to a quiff, she answers. You gonna be here, ready for me, next time I show up in this crummy town?"

"Maybe," she said, and was alarmed when his anger burst into flame and he struck the side of his palm against her neck.

"Don't you bull me!" he cried.

"Let me go now," she said, frightened.

"What're you, ganging up?"

"No, please..."

"They put you onto me. Russ and the others told you about Barney and they says to con him, yeah?"

"No..."

"Russ and the boys didn't pay you to give me the horse laugh?" he sneered. "You wasn't supposed to hand me that crud about how to treat you?"

"No."

She felt his heavy fists as he pummeled against her in the rear of the truck. He raised her into his immense hands, pitched her toward the wall and, puffing and swearing, his face brightening, clumped once more toward her. "Vicious, huh?" he rumbled.

"You want vicious, I give you vicious!" He yanked her toward him by grabbing her breasts rudely, squeezing the pink nipples, and thrusting her to the floor of the truck. Sliding away, she had no consciousness of screaming, of making a sound. She felt herself being raised again, felt the heat of his doubled fist crashing into her belly. She called out in pain, but that only enraged him further and his knee thrust at her jaw.

Sinking into unconsciousness, she still heard his hoarse breathing but she no longer could feel pain. She wondered, as the darkness enveloped her, what she had done to make him, to make anyone, this uncontrollably angry.

The sun had come up when she wakened, in the dust of the wide lot. Her chin ached and she looked down to see that her belly was a livid red. She was entirely naked. Her clothes were nearby, but they were torn almost to shreds. Her thighs were remarkably sore.

She waited as long as she could, and then looked up. The unfamiliar lot was vacant.

She could not find her purse.

She lay in the dirt and knew she never had been more undressed, more alone.

Slowly turning over, shamed by the dryness in her throat, she pushed her palms against the ground and caught a rueful glance of her breasts. They hurt terribly because he had abused them, because he had punched them.

Falling back, aware of excruciating pain she was certain would never be relieved, she wondered if she would ever come alive again.

"Daddy," she whispered. "Daddy, I need you…"

Mike was able to snag two tickets to the Monteux concert at Carnegie Hall in the city, and he and Nancy just made it to their seats by 8:30. The concert and his attentiveness thrilled her and, long before the intermission when they were herded into an alcove for cigarettes, she knew that he would spend the night with her.

She assumed he had checked with Grand Central to see when trains returned to Waymouth, but, when he seemed in no particular hurry after the concert was over, she didn't press it.

"That looks like a halfway decent bar across the street," Mike said, once they had left Carnegie. "Shall we try it?"

I don't want to sit in a stuffy bar and talk, my darling, she thought. I want you to take me to a room where there's a bed, a big, welcoming bed, and I want us to make love. The shame that shackled me for ever so long is leaving my mind and my body and I'm impatient with ceremonies. I love you and I don't want to waste a precious moment with talk, with propriety, with anything that's civilized.

I want you forever, my darling, and I'll let you take me on any terms you desire. I won't expect a wedding band because we slept together and will sleep together again. The hill girl with adolescent, happily-ever-after fantasies is no more. I love you, I love you, I love you, and I will take whatever you choose to give me.

"You're not listening, lady," Mike scolded with a smile. "Does that bar look okay?"

"Whatever you say," Nancy replied, and he took her arm.

In the bar he was obviously ill at ease, and she wondered why. They exchanged pleasant trivia over their drinks and, when it became apparent that he wanted to discuss the two of them seriously, she agreed to dismiss the safe, small talk.

Mike spoke with difficulty because his words would not pour freely and because in the background a juke box thundered a concerto which should have been played softly. He attempted to explain, after a rambling, nervous beginning, why he had taken her to bed in the first place. Nancy, as nervous as he, assured him she required no explanations, but he insisted on going on. He had married a woman who was emotionally a child, he said, a fact whose implication plagued him because the simple rule of societal thumb read that adults reserved themselves for adults, that the mature never had the need nor the urge to marry the immature. He continued haltingly, as if apologizing for a mistake in judgment he'd made long before he'd met Nancy, and for what he was convinced were the horrendous, unflattering reasons for reaching out for Nancy.

She interrupted him.

"Dearest," she said in a steady voice, "if you really knew how unimportant all that is to me now, you'd laugh out loud. Take me back to the hotel," she said, her finger tracing the veins in his hand. "Take me to bed."

They missed the last express to Waymouth but made a sooty, depressing local which seemed to stop at every other telephone pole. They were the only ones in the rattling car except for a pink-cheeked sailor and his girl, necking in the last seat.

It was very late when they stood in the hotel corridor and Mike unlocked her door, but neither of them was tired. An instant after they were in the room they were in each other's arms. Nancy gasped as he kissed her neck and her cheek and her mouth hungrily, and they lowered to her bed together, not wasting time to pull down the spread.

Nancy held his head between the palms of her hands and knew almost at once that this time was different, different from the melancholy laboredness of his drunken night, different from the extensive tenderness and tact in the motel. This time he was completely a man, her man, and he was enjoying her marvelously, loving her receptive, pliant body and showing her he was pleased when she surprised him with initiative of her own.

"My lover," she breathed again and again as he took her.

They rested for a long while later, not quite dozing. At one point—she had no idea how long afterwards—he brought her to him again, held her nearly as firmly as before, and said, "I have something to tell you, Nancy."

"More confessions?" she teased.

"No confessions, merely an announcement. I think your idea that we get married as soon as I'm free is a good one."

"My—*my* idea?"

"Well, mine then. It doesn't matter much, does it? I suppose I could court you for another half-year or so and then pop the question, but that's so much time-wasting. What do you say?"

"I—I say yes; what else did you think I'd say?" Nancy answered after what she knew was an appalling pause.

"I'm glad," he said lazily, and she had the grave suspicion that he was going to go to sleep. "I can just see it now. Ten years from now a TV interviewer will ask you, 'Mrs. Crayne, what were you doing when your husband first proposed?' "

Nancy shared his cigarette as they talked, as she did her best to see marriage with Mike Crayne not as a word game played after love-making, but as reality. When she leaned across his chest to put the cigarette into the tray, he stopped talking suddenly and once more she received him.

Drowsiness came to her and she snuggled against him. When she closed her eyes and felt his warmth, she saw stationery, with the legend *Mrs. Michael Crayne* engraved at the top.

CHAPTER SEVEN

WHEN HE first heard that the homicide bureau would subpoena the Alders' files on Julia Havilland and Marianne
Sherwood, if necessary, Phil was prepared to protest, but he
knew that in the clinches his victory would add up to nothing
more than a waiting game. In the next few days he and the others
would leave Waymouth, their survey here concluded, to set up
shop in Albany. The police's function was to investigate crime, he
had been assured, and if the Institute's records on Havilland and
Sherwood would in any way cast any light on them the police had
a right to inspect the records.

Psychologists, he also had been assured, did not by law enjoy
the same privileges of confidential relationship that the physi-
cian, psychiatrist and clergyman did. That meant that if Phil
and the team found themselves in Albany, deep in the middle of
research, and the Waymouth subpoena was workable, they could
conceivably find themselves being hailed back to Waymouth. The
police were not required to turn anything of a private nature over
to the newspapers, but the newspapers hardly relied on the police
alone for assistance. During the conduct of the initial investiga-
tion, Julia Havilland had been asked if she and Mrs. Sherwood
had been interviewed by the Alders team, and she had said yes.
The papers had not allowed that noteworthy item to slip by.

Eventually Phil agreed to meet with the court psychiatrist,
armed with all the material he had available on the women,
because he was acutely conscious of being in a bind. Two women
were involved in a slaying, the papers screeched, following

interviews with the Alders Institute Survey on Sex Conduct. If he dug into the private files and handed over the material, most potential interviewees in Albany and the other upcoming cities and towns would think twice before volunteering. If he refused to cooperate with the Waymouth Police, the newspaper jackals would be overjoyed and the stigma would still be there.

Either way, thought Phil Morrow as he tiredly paced the living room of the suite and heard his own sorry sigh, the house had fallen and would take a long time to rebuild.

To the competent, placidly friendly detective named Del-Vaille, he explained that Mrs. Sherwood and Mrs. Havilland had each been interviewed only once, that the entrance of the Alders name into the case would help the police infinitesimally and would harm the Alders Institute immeasurably. DelVaille nodded genially but was unimpressed.

The time arrived when the team was to meet with the court psychiatrist, a bespeckled gnome named Dr. Frye. Mrs. Havilland's relation to the defendent and to the crime was still vague, but the former's husband, apparently a big wheel in Waymouth insurance and real estate, had summoned a specialist from New York to treat his wife. "There is a grievous mistake," Charles Havilland was quoted as saying. "Any responsible citizen of Waymouth will swear that my wife is no more capable of taking the remotest part in violence than she is of flying. Everyone from the City Council to Reverend Pendleton already has attested to that. What more do you want? A human being's good name is better than money in the bank, and my wife has the best name ever known in Waymouth."

As for Marianne Sherwood, who once had acted in the movies, the story was considerably less muddy. Her diagnosis was inarguably hallucinatory. She had flailed at the police who had led her to confinement, she had torn her dress with her nails, had struggled to rip it off and throw it at them. She had blistered in obscene language that they had no right to detain her because her private plane was waiting for her at the airport to carry her to Hollywood. In twenty-four hours she was to report to Dayne Studios where the first day's shooting on a picture called *Lot's Wife* would begin. She was its star and if they would only contact Aaron Miles, the producer-director, she could prove it.

The police had contacted Aaron Miles, only because there was the chance she was not entirely lying. When he was reminded her screen name was Marianne Terrin, he needed time to remember her. Finally he did remember her and stated, "Miss Joanna Archer has been signed to portray the title role in *Lot's Wife*. I do happen to recall Miss Terrin. She once appeared in one of my earlier films for, I think, something like two and a half minutes on the screen. You may herewith consider it a point of fact, gentlemen, that Miss Terrinn never has been a member of the Miles squad, as we like to say, nor, as far as I am able to ascertain, any kind of contender in any other Hollywood squad. If she chooses to use my name for cheap publicity, let me—"

Waiting for the psychiatrist to contact him for the meeting, Phil went over Mike's notes on Marianne Sherwood. They were completely in order and, he discerned, their conclusions were accurate. Then he read Nelson's notes on Julia Havilland and was troubled. He had read scores of Partridge's reports before and had accepted them as reasonable gossip, chiefly because Dr. Alders had always been impressed.

Now there was a difference. The Havilland notes were demonstrably deck-stacking, as Mike had quizzically used the phrase, and, added to the suspicion of Partridge's techniques, they were damning.

When Mike returned to the suite, Phil voiced his fear.

"If I know anything about reading between lines," he said, handing the report to Mike, "that pup was doing what he assumed was treatment on Julia Havilland. And if that psychiatrist Frye suggests that Nelson in any way encouraged her to act on her latent homosexuality, the survey's in real trouble. It'll be a brushfire and the rest of us will be burned."

Mike read the notes, carefully, silently, and finally looked up. "Speaking of being burned, you could set a match to this report"

"That bad?"

"I call it irresponsible as hell. So do you. What do you imagine a psychiatrist is going to say? 'Let's canonize Partridge'? Your only out, sport, is to flush this down the john and hide the kid in a closet"

"Don't tempt me."

"Otherwise," Mike declared evenly, "you can face up to the fact that maybe you're the culprit."

"Give me that again."

"I tried to, if you'll remember, from the start. Alders did, too. If you're going to help people in trouble, you have to be available to take the responsibility for opening them up and leading them toward a cure. They always get sicker before they get better, and you were always in too much of a hurry."

"But it can work! I've seen it work! Do you know what's happened to Sally Warner since—"

"What the hell do you mean, it can work? Is every unconscious the same, can it begin functioning on schedule and follow a straight path on schedule? Nobody has a right to begin helping if he's not going to be around to see it through. You're skilled, sure, and I'm skilled, but that's only because we've learned something about discipline. You started the game. How can you blame Partridge for wanting to be an assistant Messiah?"

Phil summoned Nelson to the suite.

"You certainly are acquainted with the word 'lesbian,' Nelson," said Phil. "In such a few number of pages you've used it liberally."

Lounging in the hotel's armchair, Nelson raised a hand to suppress a yawn, but so artlessly that there was no doubt he was worried.

"Isn't that one of our rules, Phil?" Nelson asked, and smiled embarrassedly at the quiet Mike. " 'If the shoe fits' and so on and so on."

"What about Julia Havilland? Is she a lesbian?"

"You've read the newspapers. Is there any doubt?"

"I didn't ask that. I want to know about your session with her. Is she a lesbian?"

Partridge sat up and cleared his throat. "You read my report." He crossed his legs. "Dr. Alders seemed satisfied with every report I handed in. Are you dissatisfied, Phil?"

"I'm dissatisfied with the frequency of that word 'lesbian.' Not 'lesbian tendencies' or 'admittedly bisexual,' but 'lesbian.' How come? You saw her only once, for no longer than sixty minutes."

"Once? I saw her twice."

"This file says once," Phil argued and, flipping the manila envelope over, recited the date of interview.

"Oh. Well..."

"Which was it, Nelson? Once or twice?"

"Look..."

"Did you practice psychotherapy on Julia Havilland?"

"Phil, if you could have seen this pathetic woman, dripping with lesbian guilt, begging for the most slender reed to help her face her reality..."

Mike Crayne shot a glance at Phil and said, "You're 'way too rough on him, sport. Take it easy." He grinned and offered his pack of cigarettes. "Cigarette, Nelson?"

The young man seemed welcomely relieved that the heat had lessened. "You know I've never smoked, Mike," he told his new friend.

"Ever been woolly-eyed drunk?"

"Can't say that I ever have," he chuckled, "not if you make me give the Scout's Honor."

"Ever shacked up with a girl?"

He glared. "Now listen! What the devil is this? What the devil are you getting at?"

"Tell the truth, Nelson," Mike said, still grinning. "You're a nice-looking, clean-cut, normal guy who's never smoked, never been drunk, and as far as I've detected since I've known you, never been interested in girls. I'm just putting it to you as a pal. Smoke and drink are bad for the system. But haven't you ever once made some appreciable time with a girl?"

"You're acting strange, Mike."

"I don't think so. Forget Phil here. He's a great guy but he sometimes thinks he's Napoleon. I'm asking a fair question, man to man. Have you ever had a woman?"

The silence in the air was heavy before Nelson replied. "No, never." There was a queerly proud expression on his face.

"Why not?" Mike inquired, in close to a soothing whisper.

The pause was again stark. Then: "Because it's wrong. It's all wrong. It's—you'll laugh at the word, won't you?"

"Why would I laugh?"

"It's—evil."

"Sex?"

"Yes, of course, sex. Every phase of it. They wrap you around their fingers and charm you into working your head off and dying long before your time so that they can live on and on. They spur you by doling out their frigid bodies when you bring in the gifts, and they push you away when you don't. Isn't that true, Mike? Truthfully? Man to man? Isn't that what this supposedly monumental, earth-shaking thing called sex is really all about? Doling, always doling? Aren't they forever needling us to do better, to slay more dragons, to haul in bigger pelts than the Joneses?"

"They? Who's they, Nelson? All women? Wives? Mothers?"

Nelson tightened, but only for a fleck. "My mother, your mother, everybody's mother. This junk about comparing the glories of motherhood to all the other glories—oh, all of them, patriotism, corn on the cob, The Holy Mount, all of them—it's stagnated around long enough. If you want to know the truth, it's a concept that's the most dangerous of them all and it has to be exposed."

"And our survey is the means to do it."

"You asked about my mother," said Nelson, enthusiastically sitting forward, as if no one had ever asked him before. "Do you honestly want to know about my mother? And my father?"

"Yes."

"You would have liked my father. His name was Nelson Partridge, too. Nelson Alcott Partridge, the Second; I'm the Third. A finer man never lived than my father. He made his living selling typewriters in a small shop, but it brought in money enough to provide for all of us. On the side he wrote books. Wonderful books. He paid to have them printed and published because the big New York houses are a monopoly and won't read an unknown great writer's work. The books lost money. Every time those letters would come in, telling him like a slap in the face that he was a failure, do you imagine for a minute that my mother would buck him up?

"I was his son and he was crazy about me. He'd take me off to hidden corners away from her and he'd read me Dickens and Mark Twain. She'd find us. She'd always find us and give him hell for wasting my time and everybody's time, when he could be out earning lots and lots of money."

"Nelson .. ".

"You don't know what it was like. He was so wonderfully good and she was so bad. She and all her sisters, all those women with their B.O. who charged into our house on Sundays and chattered about their own husbands. They never once said a kind word. Their husbands were drinkers, they complained, and atheists and horrors and all types of weaklings."

Mike lazily spread his arms and told Phil, "You can take it from here, sport."

Closing the folder, Phil darkened and directed, "You get back to your room and pack your bags. When you've finished doing that, you go to the first railroad station and get as far away from us as you possibly can get."

Partridge shot from his chair. "What in the—"

"Under what you thought were my auspices, you've done a terrible thing, a thing I know you won't understand. Maybe we can help tape up the harm you've encouraged, but I don't think so. Anyway, beat it fast. I'll beat the living hell out of you if you don't."

"Do you know what you're doing?"

"There's nothing I've ever known more."

The telephone rang and Phil was asked to be in Dr. Frye's office, with records, within an hour.

"I'll tag along this time, if it'll help," Mike offered.

"No, thanks," Phil replied. "I was the one who rolled the snowball down the hill; it's up to me to see where it lands."

"Don't look all that glum, sport. It may be rugged sailing for a while, but we're not through yet. One foul-up, if that's what they decide to call it, won't bust us. The Institute still makes all the sense it always did. You'll have plenty of professionals to back you up."

"That's mighty fine graveyard whistling, partner. But what if we do get busted? Can you make plans for yourself?"

"I've made one fairly important plan already, if you'll come along as best man. Nancy's going to be my child bride."

"Well, what do you know!" Phil exclaimed and extended his hand.

"Not much, except that I was a damn fool for not noticing her sooner. Of course, the divorce has to come through, but that shouldn't take forever."

"You're a lucky mug. So is Nancy."

"Yeah, she keeps telling me." Mike rose to get Phil's brief-case, and brought it to him. "Just remember what Pappy tells you, pal. The newspapers are going to try to nail us to the stake, but we have the best gawddamn outfit on land and foam. We'll beat this."

Just before Phil left, the telephone called him back and he heard Sally Warner's voice. He sensed immediately that she was disturbed.

She needed room and time to tell him why she was disturbed and Phil gave them to her. Once she began, she told him a story he could not wholly understand because she digressed and apol-ogized and at several points seemed to be struggling to catch her breath, but the gist of it soon became clear, bitterly clear. As he had feared in some far-off semiconscious way last night as they'd talked, she had not stayed in her hotel room. She had gone to the worst section of town, where she had picked up a man who had helped her prove she was a hopeless slut by slipping her a hate called love and then beating her up.

"Why did you take so long to call me?" Phil demanded, con-fident that he sounded like neither a nag nor an I-told-you-As so he parent. waited for her to form her words he read his wrist watch and fervently hoped her slow speech wouldn't place him in a hateful position of rushing her.

"It was the queerest thing," she admitted finally, speaking cautiously but no longer interrupting herself. "I couldn't seem to move from there, even after the sun came up and I knew that sooner or later someone would see me. My money was gone—the little I had and all you gave me—and my...my clothes were—torn."

The phone appeared to go dead for a time. "Go on, Sally," Phil said patiently, caring, wishing he could steer a racing truck into the truck driver and all the truck drivers who believed waifs when they said they wanted to be bums.

"There's a girl I went to school with—her name is Eileen Shepherd now—and I remembered she and her husband live in Lassiterville. I knew she wouldn't ask me a million questions if I asked her not to. I—went to her house, as soon as I could get myself together. I walked there through all the back roads I knew, but some people saw me. I think I recognized one of them, or I mean I think one of them recognized me, but I kept going. Eileen let me come in. She was just on her way to work. Her husband Ronnie'd already left. I told her a little bit, but not much. She put me right to bed and brought me some warm milk. I fell asleep. I just woke up."

"Sally," Phil said, "now listen to me. Can you stay there, say, for another couple of hours? Alone, I mean? I was about to tell you to come here and wait for me to get back, but it's better that you stay with friends, or at least in the home of friends. I can't come to you now but I can soon. Can you wait for me?"

"Yes," she replied falteringly, "but—"

"Do that. Please believe me, Sally, I'd come to you right away if I possibly could, but it's impossible. Sally, do you hear me?"

" ... I let us all down, didn't I?"

"Let us down?"

"You made such wonderful sense last night," she said. "I swear I meant to stay at The Bromley, to let what you told me sink in, but all the time that you gave me was no use, was it? I'm not the—person I wanted to be, the grown-up, decent person. What happened shows it. I'll never—"

"That's what we'll talk about soon, Sally. The fact that you wanted and still want to be a grown-up, decent person is what counts. I told you that yesterday and it still goes." He purposely talked more quietly when he added, "Will you listen to something else?"

"Yes."

"I've witnessed and heard and examined scores on scores of people with trouble, people who've finally made the grade. And do you know my conclusion? It's just about physically impossible to make lasting progress without setbacks.

"Wait for me, Sally," he said after he jotted down her friends' address. "I don't have to tell you you did the wrong thing, but I do have to tell you that you don't have as far to go toward becoming that grown-up, decent person as you think."

In the taxi, Phil was worried about the call he would have to pay on Mrs. Alders, about the direct or indirect meetings he would have with Soren and Rothschild and all the rest They would radiate with doctorates, their jargon would be right out of the Case of Dora, and they would let the world know he had come a scientific cropper. He had been handed the instruments of professional experiment by a man surely his master and, according to them, he had failed.

Only a handful of tabloids were needed now to highlight the word "failure."

He knew what was coming.

As the cab turned a Waymouth corner, Phil Morrow thought of Sally Warner, and that helped a little.

Her conflicts were serious but aboveboard, almost ingenuous. There would be no drawn-out treatment required for Sally, no hushed hospital walls, no grim nurses with gum shoes and restrictions. Basically she was sound as a dollar, far and away sounder than the scads of wretchedly restless dollars he and Mike had met. And would meet in the future.

Her prognosis was good, perhaps excellent. He conceived of her sister helping her move her belongings out of the house, of her father doing little more than ranting and ineffectually striving to call her back. There was no reason she wouldn't agree to get professional help, to which Phil would lend his most supportive assistance.

Albany was not that far from Manhattan. Eventually it was very possible she could come to call him Phil.

He emerged from the taxi, paid his fare, and thought, Mike Crayne is right. We'll beat this. And if we don't, then we'll start again—not from scratch, because too much that's good has already been invested.

He entered the building and gave his name to the man at the desk.